ST BRIGID'S
BOUNCES BACK

ABOUT THE AUTHOR

Geri Valentine was born in Dublin and now lives near Dundalk, Co Louth. *St Brigid's Bounces Back* is the third book in the hugely successful St Brigid series which includes *Bad Habits at St Brigid's* and *New Broom at St Brigid's*.

ST BRIGID'S
BOUNCES BACK

GERI VALENTINE

POOLBEG

Published in 1994 by
Poolbeg Press Ltd,
Knocksedan House,
123 Baldoyle Industrial Estate,
Dublin 13, Ireland

© Geri Valentine 1994

The moral right of the author has been asserted.

A catalogue record for this book is available from the British Library.

ISBN 1 85371 415 1

Cover by Marie Louise Fitzpatrick
Cover design by Poolbeg Group Services Ltd
Set by Poolbeg Group Services Ltd in Stone 9.5/13
Printed by Cox & Wyman Ltd, Reading, Berks.

For Madeline & Miriam with love

Contents

Prologue

It was very silent in the moonlit garden. Fragrant clusters of white jasmine gleamed among the dark foliage scrambling up the walls, and intertwining with the profusion of thorny roses, heavy with silken blooms.

A man sat immobile on an elaborately carved stone seat, seemingly untouched by all the scented beauty around him. The iron gate in the wall close by opened. A voice speaking low and clear broke the silence.

"The doctor confirms it. The old man is seriously ill. Go and get the girl now, Mahmoud. The time is right. PR is in London to assist you."

For the first time the man on the stone seat moved. He got up and looked at the other framed in the gateway.

"I go. You are sure she is somewhere in Ireland?"

"Yes, that much is certain."

Mahmoud moved towards the gate. When he had passed through it, the other man closed it carefully behind him, then swiftly returned back to where he had come from.

1

Return Journey

"Good grief," exclaimed Nuala poking in a rucksack inscribed Cool Cat. "I must have left the wretched things behind after all."

Mrs O'Donnell carefully overtook a grey Jaguar which was travelling abnormally slow for a car of its calibre.

"What things?" she asked absently. "Nothing important I hope. We are too far from home to go back now."

"No, they're not important. Just batteries for Judith's radio and my torch. I like to have a torch in the dorm. I only bought them yesterday. I left them on the hall table 'specially so I wouldn't forget them today, idiot that I am," confessed Nuala crossly.

"Don't worry, Nuala, I'm not that fussed about my radio. Somehow I have never much time to listen to it at school anyway. There's always so much going on," was Judith's response from the back of the car.

Nuala laughed and turned around in her seat. "Thanks, Ju, but as it's only two PM now, we can

\text{}

stop at a shop on our way. If you don't mind, Mum."

"As long as you're quick about it. I want to get to St Brigid's and home again before it gets dark. If I remember rightly there's quite a big shop a few miles down this road. We'll stop there."

"Great, Mum. Isn't it weird, Ju, going back to school late like this, and all because we were invited to Bill Crilly's wedding?" Bill Crilly, brother of the school's science teacher, had become very friendly with Nuala and Judith the previous term, helping them not only to solve the mystery of a secret passage in St Brigid's, but also to catch the thieving intruder who had been using it.

"We haven't missed much," replied Judith. "I still can't believe Bill and Anne are married, they only met a few months ago."

"I don't suppose they would have got married so quickly only for that job in Mexico. Bill didn't want to wait a whole year. It was nice of them to ask us though. We have loads to tell the others."

"Anne looked fabulous, didn't she? I liked the bridesmaid's dress too; dark blue really suited her," said Judith in a dreamy voice.

"I don't know how they managed to arrange the wedding so quickly," replied Nuala's mother, "But I agree with you Judith, Anne looked simply lovely."

"I wonder will Miss Crilly miss Bill much?" asked Nuala with interest. "She'll have no one to share the house with now."

"Maybe Mike Greene will get friendly with her," observed Judith with a giggle.

3

"Hardly, not after that terrible row they had at the wedding," giggled Nuala in turn. "When I saw that he was best man I had hopes they might make a match of it but I'm afraid there's no chance of that now."

"I'm fond of Bill but I'm glad he's gone to Mexico," pronounced Mrs O'Donnell unexpectedly. "Perhaps with him gone St Brigid's will revert to being an ordinary school again."

"That's not fair," protested Nuala. "It wasn't Bill's fault at all. He only got caught up in it to help us."

"That's what you say, but if he hadn't encouraged you, you wouldn't have gone ahead the way you did. Anyway, it's got to stop now and I mean it."

"But Mum," protested Nuala yet again. "What else could we have done? It's not like you to be so unreasonable and it's all ended well."

"That's not the point, Nuala. You should have gone straight to Sr Gobnait and left it to her. She's more than capable of taking care of any situation."

Nuala sighed. "But Mum . . . " then she shrugged her shoulders and let it go. *Mothers*, she thought. Judith threw her a glance of understanding and sympathy.

There was silence in the car until a large shop came into sight. Mrs O'Donnell drove almost to the shop door.

"Don't be long now," she warned. "Do you need money?"

Nuala shook her head and got out of the car

followed by Judith.

As Nuala pushed the shop door open, she confided to Judith, "I wonder has anyone been getting at Mum? It's not like her to go on like that."

"It's funny all right, I suppose she worries about you," Judith replied as they walked around the empty shop.

It didn't take them long to find the batteries. Then Judith decided she needed some stationery, stamps and a packet of crisps.

By the time they got to the checkout a tall thin man had come into the shop and was standing stooped over the assistant there, talking earnestly to her. When the girl saw Judith and Nuala in their striped school blazers waiting with their purchases, she smiled at them.

"You're from St Brigid's aren't you? I wonder could you help the professor here . . . " she asked. "He's looking for the *Boyne Arms.*"

"Professor PR Jenkins," enunciated the tall man, lifting a battered antiquarian hat from his head. His mild eyes looked anxiously at them from his bespectacled face.

"He's down for the fishing," explained the assistant with the voice of one who felt that the fishes had nothing much to worry about.

"No problem," replied Nuala cheerfully. "It's on our way, Professor, if you follow us we'll lead you to it."

"Thank you very much, my dear young lady," he beamed at her. "My car is outside the door."

They paid their bill and went out of the shop, followed by the Professor. Nuala hastily explained the situation to her mother, who assured Professor Jenkins that she would be only too happy to oblige him. Protesting his thanks he doddered off to his car which to Nuala's and Judith's surprise turned out to be a Jaguar.

"He didn't look that sort of person at all," Judith remarked to Nuala as Mrs O'Donnell drove away from the shop.

"You're right. I thought he'd be the old battered station wagon sort," agreed Nuala.

"What a pair you are!" Mrs O'Donnell was amused. "He seemed quite ordinary to me."

"That's what we meant," explained Nuala kindly. "Jags are usually driven by dashing hunks, not old buffers like him."

"That's not a nice way to speak of anyone," reproved her mother. "Especially a professor – what of, I wonder?"

"He didn't say," replied Nuala losing interest in the conversation as she munched some of the crisps which Judith had passed to her.

Having successfully steered Professor Jenkins to the *Boyne Arms* Nuala's mother put on a bit of speed and managed to reach the school by four pm.

As Nuala was about to get out of the car and remove her cases from the boot, her mother stopped her.

"Wait Nuala, I've something to say to you." Nuala closed the door again and looked at Mrs

O'Donnell. "Sr Gobnait sent all the parents a letter explaining that a firm of experts came down from Dublin and went over the whole castle. They made sure there wasn't even one secret entrance left."

"Thank goodness, I never liked the thought of a secret entrance. I suppose that fall of rocks we heard must have blocked up the passages," remarked Nuala.

"Probably, anyway they've checked and cross-checked every teacher in the school too, so that there should be no more escapades this term, thank goodness. I want you to settle down and work for a change. If you see or hear anything unusual, please report it at once to Sr Gobnait. That's her responsibility, and to be fair, she wishes you to leave it to her. I don't want you caught up in any more adventures, do you understand?"

"I thought somebody had got at you," observed Nuala with satisfaction, nodding at Judith as she spoke. "Anyway Mum don't worry. I won't have time to do any rescuing or sleuthing this term as I shall be devoting my time to the history essay competition. I mean to win a prize, preferably first prize." With that she kissed her mother and got out of the car, followed by Judith, who had remained to express her thanks to Nuala's mother.

There was nobody about when the girls, having waved Mrs O'Donnell on her way, arrived at Sr Gobnait's office. However they could see a dormitory list on the nearby notice-board, and eagerly scanned the neat rows of names there. To their delight they were back in St Ita's dormitory, along with Josie, Aileen, the twins, Gwendoline, Monica and Deirdre O'Reilly.

"Brilliant!" cried Judith. "We're all back together again."

"What's come over the Major? Anyway let's get up to the dorm and get our cubes fixed up. We can report to the boss later," suggested Nuala.

"Right," replied Judith cheerfully. "Lead on, O'Donnell."

So they picked up their cases, bags and various bits and pieces once again and proceeded up the familiar staircase to the dormitory.

They had hardly finished making their beds and arranging their belongings when the dormitory door burst open and Aileen and the two Murrays almost fell in, all excitement and laughter.

"Welcome back, welcome back," they chanted unmelodiously.

"You are back, aren't you?" called Eithne, rushing over to Judith's cubicle and looking in.

"Hi Eithne," Judith greeted her cousin affectionately. Holding up a big soft brightly-coloured toy lion she said, "Meet Goldie – isn't he perfect?" before placing him carefully against her pillows.

Nuala strolled over to join them. "Hi Aileen, Hi Fidelma," she greeted them. "Who sleeps here?" she asked indicating an empty cubicle beside her own.

"We don't know," replied Fidelma. "The bed is made and everything hung up and arranged, but nobody knows who it's for."

"Strange, it's a funny time of the year for new

8

girls to come, don't you think?" Nuala pointed out.

"Maybe Tara is coming after all," suggested Judith. Tara was a teenage actress who appeared in the *Jungle* ads on TV, one of which had been filmed in St Brigid's during the previous term. Aileen had made friends with her then, and they still corresponded with each other.

Aileen shook her head. "Definitely not. I had a letter yesterday. She really wanted to come here, but her mother thought we would be too quiet and countrified. She preferred one of the big Dublin schools. Anyway the latest news is that they've dropped the whole idea and Tara's off to France to make a film."

"A film! I didn't know Tara was interested in films," remarked Judith.

"She is, so there'll be no more *Jungle* ads this year," Aileen said sadly.

"Hi Ju, hi Nuala!" came Josie's voice from the door. "It's great to see you back again. I'm dying to hear about the wedding."

She came into the room. "I have a message for you. The head girl wants us all to go to the sixth year common room at five pm. She's holding a special meeting of the history club. She didn't say, but I gather they're eager to hear about the wedding, too."

"Great. Has she anything interesting to tell us?" asked Judith eagerly.

Josie shook her head. "I don't know any more than that. You don't have long to wait, it's nearly five already."

"Are you ready, Judith?" asked Nuala. "I think we'd better report to dear old Gobberlets before we go to the common room."

"Just a min. I have to get my drawing things. I want to leave them in the art room on the way down," Judith replied.

"I'm amazed at you keeping up art after all the fuss of last term," teased Nuala.

Judith grinned. "I learned a lot last term, you know. I hope Sr Patrick is as good a teacher as Mrs McGlade was."

"Did you hear about the new tennis coach?" Josie asked Nuala as they led the way downstairs.

"Mr Honeycombe," replied Nuala. "What's he like?"

"Well . . . tall . . . bronzed . . . very fit . . . and he wants us all to call him Steve."

Nuala looked impressed.

Aileen who had caught up with them added her bit. "The sixth years are nuts on him. I heard Jocelyn tell Sharon Kennedy that he reminded her of Kevin Costner."

"Kevin Costner! I must see this hunk, is he any good at tennis?"

"I suppose so, he's played at Wimbledon several times. He hasn't coached us yet. We have him on Thursday next."

"Is the new swimming pool in use yet?" asked Nuala when they reached the ground floor. Judith and her cousins left them then, and went on to go to the art room.

"No. It's taking a long time, isn't it?" replied

Josie. "The rumour is that they haven't enough money to fund it."

"Labour costs went up or something," agreed Aileen.

They walked along to Sr Gobnait's office where Judith joined them. Nuala and Judith went in to report while Aileen and Josie walked slowly ahead. The twins, who were not members of the history club, had gone off on business of their own.

Sr Gobnait didn't keep them long and they soon caught up with the other two. The school clock struck five as they opened the door of the sixth year common room.

"Good," said Mary Jones when she saw the four third years come into the room. "We are all here now. Grab a seat everyone and sit down."

The twenty members of the history club disposed themselves around the available chairs. Sharon Kennedy, a bossy fifth year, threw a few cushions over to Judith, which she shared with Aileen. Nuala and Josie perched themselves on the arms of two old battered armchairs, which were occupied by Jocelyn O'Leary and Maeve Byrne, both sixth years.

The head girl stood up and announced: "I've called this meeting because I'm afraid the club will have to be dropped for the summer term. The Leaving Cert looms horribly large and none of us sixth years can spare time from our study. Anyway Sr Gobnait has something new up her sleeve. It's a club called Boynepeace, and some of it will be a joint effort with Newgrange College."

11

She smiled at the excited buzz of talk which rose from the listening girls.

"Who'll be taking the club?" asked Aileen.

"Miss Crilly and Miss Ryan here, and I believe a Mr Greene who is a teacher in Newgrange," was the answer.

"Oh no," cried Nuala and Judith simultaneously. "Not *Mike Greene!*"

"Why not?" asked a greatly surprised Mary. "Do you know him?"

"Well," replied Nuala, "he was best man at Bill Crilly's wedding and the bride and groom had hardly left for Dublin airport when he and Miss Crilly had a blazing row."

"Oh no," gasped the head girl, while a series of "What was the row about?" rose from around the room.

"I don't really know," confessed Nuala. "Judith and I weren't there when it started but I believe they hadn't been speaking since they appeared at the church."

"Well that should liven things up a bit for the club," laughed Sharon. "Perhaps you'll have to change the name."

"I'm sure it will have blown over by the time you have the first meeting," said Mary repressively, glancing reprovingly at Sharon. "Now Nuala and Judith, we want to hear all about the wedding, omitting no detail however slight. Start at the very beginning."

2

Dark Stranger

"Gwendoline O'Hagan, what are you doing?" asked Miss Ryan testily, looking at the back row where all she could see of Gwendoline was an upraised desk lid.

"Getting my history book out," answered Gwendoline as she quickly stuffed *Fashion and Flair* magazine out of sight. She closed the desk and waved her textbooks at the teacher.

"Judging from the first draft of your work for the history competition," the teacher pointed out dryly, "it looks as if you need to spend a lot more time studying your history books."

"But Miss Ryan," replied Gwendoline earnestly, "I really worked hard on it during the holidays."

"Maybe you did. But to describe tenth century men and women as bad dressers and never in fashion even for that century wasn't very accurate. Where did you get that idea from anyway?"

"It was this marvellous book Mummy got for me called *Clothes and Customs in Ancient Times*," replied Gwendoline, enjoying herself. "There was a picture in it of a tenth century Irish woman and

13

her man. Miss Ryan, you couldn't believe how awful their clothes were, really old hat and so dim, even the Normans' funny ribbed tights looked better, though not much," she sniggered.

Miss Ryan sighed deeply. "Maybe you're right, Gwendoline. Anyway, I've marked some suggestions in your copy and I would be glad if you paid attention to them."

She picked up a pile of copy books, handing them to a red-haired girl in the front row. "Deirdre, please distribute these to their owners," she requested pleasantly.

As Deirdre handed the copies around the desks, Judith absentmindedly wondered if Miss Ryan ever missed Mrs McGlade who had been art teacher the previous term. They had shared a house after all and were always nipping up to Dublin in the latter's white Fiat. She shared with Miss Lawless now, who taught Maths. She seemed nice but then you never knew with teachers, did you?

These musings were brought to an abrupt end by the sound of Miss Ryan's voice. "Sr Francis," she announced, "is taking her class to the museum in Dublin on Wednesday afternoon. If any of you want to go with her, give in your names today. Several of you would probably find a visit there helpful for your essay, especially Nuala."

That afternoon, as the third years were strolling back to the castle after a science lesson, Judith asked Nuala, "Why did Miss Ryan think that you should go to the museum?"

Nuala looked at her in surprise. "Didn't I tell you

about the *Canticle of a Chalice*? It's my history essay which tells a strange and wonderful story of the adventures of a chalice. As there are some famous examples of chalices in the museum, I suppose Miss Ryan thinks it would be a good idea if I went and looked at them."

"What's a canticle?" asked Aileen before Judith could reply.

"It's a fancy name for a song," replied Nuala severely. "Haven't you heard of the *Canticle of Canticles* or *Song of Songs*? It's in the Bible. Really, Aileen!"

Aileen wasn't impressed. "The trouble with you, Nuala, is that you read too much," she retorted with spirit. "You'd need to watch it, one of these days your head will burst or something."

"Go on, Aileen," laughed Josie. "You're just jealous, admit it."

They had reached the school door by now. As they were about to go in Sharon Kennedy looked out. "Nuala, Sr Gobnait wants you at once," she barked crisply at her, then vanished back through the door again.

"She's got very bossy lately, hasn't she?" grumbled Aileen. "You'd think she was a teacher instead of only a fifth year."

"I wonder what Gobnait wants me for . . . " Nuala was puzzled. "I haven't had time to do anything much. I'd better go and find out. See you later."

She ran ahead, along the passage and up the stairs. As she neared the office she could see the tall nun talking to a girl about her own age. Although the girl was dressed in the school uniform, she was strange to Nuala.

"Ah Nuala," Sr Gobnait smiled benignly down at her as she approached. She drew her companion forward and Nuala was struck by a pair of brown eyes, a tanned complexion and black hair which fell in one long thick tail over one shoulder.

"This is Natalie Frossart, I want you to take special care of her. She has never been away to school before. When I say 'special care', I mean it. Make her one of your gang." Noticing the look on Nuala's face, she laughed. "You don't think I haven't noticed that you lead Aileen, Judith, Josie and the Murray twins by the nose? Now take poor Natalie in charge too, she's very shy."

"Yes, sister," replied Nuala revolted by Sr Gobnait's remarks.

"Splendid, Nuala. Off you go, Natalie," the tall nun said bracingly before she vanished back into her office.

Nuala decided to grin and bear it. "Come on, Natalie," she urged her in a friendly voice. "There's just time before tea to meet what Major Gobnait calls my gang – you'd think we were kids."

At that Natalie gave Nuala an expressive look from her big eyes, which instantly dismissed from Nuala's mind the idea that the new girl was either shy or timid.

Nuala took Natalie to the common room. As they went along she told her all she could about the school, winding up with, "Don't worry,

Natalie, you'll have the four of us, not to mention the twins – anything you want to know, just ask."

Natalie said nothing but just looked thoughtfully at her. The common room was almost completely empty but Nuala was relieved to see Aileen, Judith and Josie watching television.

"Hi chucks," she called cheerfully. "This is Natalie. The Major has asked us to look after her 'specially well'."

Josie and Aileen swivelled around in their seats and shouted "Hi" before turning back to *Aliens* which was a fascinating soap about beings trying to get on with each other in outer space. Judith, however got up and joined the newcomers.

"Hi Natalie," she said in her pleasant way. "You must be the mystery girl in our dorm."

Nuala grinned as she saw the startled look on Natalie's face. "She's talking about the cube next to mine, it's all ready for someone and we were wondering who the someone would be."

Natalie never said anything but just stared around the common room, taking in the well-worn couches and armchairs, the battered table between the windows and the row of presses which lined one wall.

Nuala, feeling a little strained, was about to ask if Sr Gobnait had omitted to mention a vital fact about the new girl, when mercifully she spoke. "What a strange place St Brigid's is, so incredibly old-fashioned and cut off from everywhere."

Her melodious voice and foreign intonation came as a shock to the other girls. Aileen jumped up from her seat and stood beside Nuala.

"It's not far away from anywhere really," she explained. "It just feels like that. Judith is from London and she thought like you once, didn't you, Ju?"

"I did indeed. I remember thinking that nothing must have happened here for centuries. Dullsville – but how wrong I was."

The others laughed as they remembered certain events which had occurred in the school the previous year.

"Where was your last school and what was it like?" asked Josie, intrigued by Natalie's face and voice.

"It was in Scotland, very big, modern, co-educational, the opposite to here," replied Natalie coolly. "Do you have much bullying?"

"We don't have any bullying here," Nuala replied. "As far as I know anyway."

Natalie looked sceptical. "All schools, even the nicest, have bullies. Everyone knows that," she stated unequivocally.

"We had a bit of bullying from the special prefects last term," Judith remarked thoughtfully, "but when Sr Gobnait discovered it, she disbanded them. Now we've only the normal prefects again."

Just then the common room door opened and a crowd of third years trooped in chattering happily and even singing. Before Nuala even had time to introduce Natalie, this crowd had surrounded the new girl, admiring her hair and her accent. Gwendoline's rather high-pitched voice could be heard informing her that she had arrived at a great time in the school year, as they would soon have a new swimming pool, latest design, of course, but also a tennis coach who had once got to the quarter-finals in Wimbledon.

Nuala, watching Natalie's animated face and gesticulating hands as she answered all the questions directed at her, wondered not for the first time why Sr Gobnait ever thought that Natalie was a shy girl who needed special attention.

"I wonder why the Major thought she was shy," Nuala confided in Aileen and Judith standing beside her.

"I can't imagine," answered Judith. "If you ask me, she's revelling in all the attention she's getting."

"That's it, now I know!" exclaimed Nuala indignantly. "She was indulging in a massive dose of the sulks because she was sent to St B's and Sr Gobnait who thinks she knows everything, confused it with shyness and timidity."

"You're right. It looks as if there's going to be a cuckoo in St Ita's this term." Aileen's tone was pessimistic. "Just when we've all got back together too."

3

Plots and Plans

"It's so hot," complained Deirdre coming into the locker room where everyone was changing for tennis. "It's shorts for me today. I'd die in a tracksuit."

"Great minds think alike," laughed Aileen who had followed her in through the door. "Look around you, not a tracksuit in sight."

"I wouldn't mind if the sun was even shining but it's just deadly hot and sticky. I thought Maths class would never end, I didn't take in one bit of all that stuff about VAT and percentages," grumbled Deirdre as she pulled her Aertex over her head.

"I was told that it rained all the time in Ireland," Natalie informed them. "It hasn't rained once since I came here."

"If you want rain, you'll get it soon. The global warming is melting the icecaps and we'll soon have rain enough to satisfy anyone," prophesied Deirdre gloomily, picking up her racquet and leaving the room.

Nuala sat down and quickly changed her shoes.

"Poor Deirdre, she always feels the heat dreadfully, maybe it's because she's got red hair."

"Why did she say I wanted rain? I adore the heat," said Natalie complacently. "If she is so hot why don't you take her for a midnight swim? It would be cool fun."

Though everyone was surprised at this suggestion they didn't find fault with it.

"It would be brilliant," agreed Josie excitedly.

Nuala shook her head. "The swimming pool isn't finished yet and the river is definitely not on."

Natalie shrugged her shoulders petulantly. "Goody-goody Nuala," she taunted as she sauntered out of the room.

Though Nuala flushed angrily, she said nothing, just opened her locker and took out her racquet and three white tennis balls. When she spoke again it was in her usual light-hearted fashion.

"Come on chucks, let's go, I'm dying to meet Steve, the wonder coach I've heard so much about."

As they approached the tennis courts Steve could be seen playing a fast game with a sixth year, June O'Reilly, who was also number one on the school team.

They joined the rest of their year who were grouped to one side of the court in question, eagerly watching the play. Suddenly the coach wound up the game with a series of brilliant shots, which even June found unreturnable. Then to Nuala's amazement he vaulted lightly over the tennis net and shook hands with June, thanking

21

her extravagantly for the game. A deep sigh of appreciation rose from the watching girls.

"He always does that," Aileen whispered to Nuala beside her. "Isn't he something?"

Nuala looked over at Steve whose tan was set off by immaculate white shorts, then she noticed that his thick hair gleaming in the light was fair.

"I thought he was supposed to look like Kevin Costner," she whispered back. "He's tall all right, but Kevin Costner's hair is dark, not fair."

Aileen shook her head vigorously. "I never said that," she protested. "I only heard Jocelyn say it, but you've got to admit he's not a bad substitute."

"Well as far as looks go, he certainly is," admitted Nuala. "But is he any good at coaching, that's the question."

She had hardly finished speaking when word was passed along that they were to form into two groups. When this was accomplished the new coach stood before them.

"Hi third years. I'm Steven Honeycoombe, just call me Steve," he began. "I want group A on my right to go off and practise on the other courts, Group B stay here. I'm going to show you how to improve your backhand stroke. We'll switch over in thirty minutes."

Nuala and Aileen found themselves in group A, teaming up with Monica and Gwendoline. While the latter pair were tossing a pound coin to see which of them would have first service, Nuala had the leisure to observe the players in the next court. Tapping Aileen on the arm she silently pointed to where Natalie was sending down lightning serves to Eithne who looked as if she was finding it hard to see them, much less return them.

Nuala raised her eyebrows.

Aileen responded with, "A dark horse, if you ask me."

"Nuala and Aileen!" called Gwendoline impatiently. "Are you two going to play today or not?"

"Sorry, Gwendoline," they replied meekly as they turned back to their own court.

It wasn't long before it was time for the groups to switch places. Steve gave group A a short demonstration on technique. Then they all had to line up and take turns in attempting to play shots against him. Nuala and Aileen managed to acquit themselves quite well, but everyone was outshone by Natalie. Even Steve was impressed with her performance. When the bell rang about twenty minutes later, nobody was surprised when Natalie received the coach's handshake, after his usual vault over the net.

Later on that day, as Nuala was writing her name down for a place on the coach which was taking the first years to Dublin, she was joined by Aileen and Judith.

"I don't think I'll go," Aileen informed her. "It's much too hot."

"You'll keep an eye on Natalie then?" asked Nuala. "She has no interest in museums either. What about you, Judith?"

"I think I'll stay here too. You don't mind, do

you, Nuala? I'll help Aileen to watch Natalie."

Nuala was quite used to going to Dublin for singing lessons without the others, so she could sincerely answer cheerfully, "No, I don't mind. We'll probably die in Dublin in this heat, but I think it's worth going."

Eithne came up and looked at the list. "Great, Nuala!" she cried. "I'm going too, we'll have each other."

"I don't envy Nuala and Eithne going to Dublin with that lot, especially in this heat," stated Judith to Aileen as they stood in front of the castle the following afternoon. They gave a last wave to the departing coach containing Sr Francis, the first years, Nuala and Eithne, and turned back into the building again.

"I think they're mad, myself, wasting a half-day in a stuffy old museum being shoved around by Sr Fusspot Francis," agreed Aileen frankly. "But Nuala's gone nuts on winning that competition."

"We promised Nuala we'd keep an eye on Natalie," Judith reminded her as they walked in a leisurely way up the stairs to the common room. "Let's find her and take her out to Barney. It'll be lovely and cool under the canopy of green leaves, listening to the river and the sound of birds and thinking beautiful thoughts."

Aileen laughed. "You're so artistic, Judith. I expect Natalie's watching *Together and Apart* with the rest of our year. Somehow I never feel like watching it now since Tara gave up those *Jungle* ads."

"*Together and Apart*, I'd forgotten all about it," sighed Judith. She looked at her watch. "It hasn't started long, maybe we'll catch the second half of it if we hurry." Then noticing the look on Aileen's face she added, "If Natalie's not there I won't bother watching it. It's too hot for TV anyway."

When they reached the common room they found not only Natalie, but Josie and Fidelma totally engrossed in watching their favourite soap, with the rest of the year.

Together and Apart was nearly over. Judith and Aileen, perched on the arm of Josie's chair, were really only in time to hear Margi scream at Joss once again, "You're grounded and this time it's indefinitely!" when the programme faded.

Deirdre got up and switched off the set. Most of the other girls got up and drifted out of the room talking and laughing.

"Hi Natalie," called Aileen grabbing her arm as she passed. Josie and Fidelma came over and joined them.

"We want to show you Barney," Judith explained. Natalie looked pleased.

"Brilliant," said Josie. "I've crisps in my locker. I'll just run down and get them. You go ahead, I'll catch up," and she rushed out of the room.

The others weren't far behind and soon Judith, leading the little procession through the wood beyond the castle garden, arrived at an enormous beech tree, its spreading branches thick with leaves.

"This is Barney, our special tree," Judith informed Natalie proudly.

"It's colossal, gigantic!" cried Natalie impressed for once. "I've never seen anything like it, those branches are so big and wide."

"Come on up," invited Judith climbing swiftly ahead, concealing her pleasure at the look of respect on Natalie's face.

"There's a fabulous view of the river from up there," Aileen informed Natalie as she and Fidelma gave the new girl a hand climbing Barney. As soon as they were seated comfortably on some of the wide branches high in the tree Josie could be heard climbing up.

"What do you think?" she asked breathlessly as she pulled herself up on the branch beside Judith. "I was passing the notice-board and what do you think was on it?"

They all stared at her.

"Well?" asked Fidelma impatiently. "What was on it?"

Josie took a deep breath. "The first Boynepeace club field outing will be next Monday morning," she announced excitedly. "It will be to Calfe's Pool to study the wildlife there. Notebooks and Biros to be taken by order of A Crilly."

"Where's this place, something's pool?" asked Natalie.

"You know the river here is called the Boyne?" explained Josie. "Well St Brigid's stretches for quite a few miles along the Boyne, our land actually goes right down to it in places. One of these places is called Calfe's Pool after some ancient old owner of the castle hundreds of years ago."

"It's very wild and woody for miles around there, though a road goes through it," added Fidelma. "I'm not surprised Miss Crilly picked it for an outing."

"I'm looking forward to it," said Judith. "We might see something interesting like a badger or a fox maybe."

Fidelma shook her head. "They only go out at night."

"I know that," replied Judith, "but you never know – in a quiet deserted spot like that anything could happen."

"If the weather is as hot as today, it will be a brilliant way to spend a morning," argued Aileen who hadn't much interest in wildlife usually.

"I must tell Miss Crilly that we have a Boynepeace enthusiast," teased Judith.

Aileen laughed. "Friday week is Nuala's birthday, any ideas for it?" she asked.

"What about a midnight feast?" suggested Natalie. "Candlelight and ghost stories. Wouldn't that be a good idea?"

"It sounds great. We've never had a midnight feast." Josie liked the idea.

"Where will we hold it, in the dorm?" asked Fidelma.

"No, not the dorm – the castle roof, the battlements," suggested Josie. "I've never been there."

"I'm not surprised." Fidelma's tone was sarcastic. "No one is ever allowed on the roof. The door to the battlements is always locked."

Aileen surprised them by announcing, "Actually I was taken up there once by Sr Clare, I can't remember why. We went up through the door which is usually locked, and some stairs and through a kind of glass building onto the roof. The roof itself is surrounded by very high walls with big slits in them. Sr Clare said they used to fire arrows or bullets through them in the old days. The nuns go up there, I remember a few wooden benches against the walls, I suppose they sit on them."

"I would like to see the roof," Josie said in a stubborn voice. "We've unlocked doors before, come on gang, let's do it again."

"Why not?" agreed Aileen. "We'll invite the whole dorm, that'll be ten of us, and give Nuala a surprise party."

"Yes, we could collect candles and stick them in jamjars or bottles and Eithne could tell one of her *Collier the Robber* stories, she knows lots."

Natalie clapped her hands. "It will be exciting!" she cried. "Something different."

Aileen got carried away and promised to make a birthday cake herself.

"A cake? You mean make it here in school?" Judith asked.

"Of course I mean to make it in school," replied Aileen proudly.

"I bet you fifty pence you can't make a cake!" Josie rashly challenged her.

"Done!" cried Aileen. "Anyone else willing to take the fifty pence bet?" She glanced around at the other girls who nodded back at her. "That's two quid. I'm sure I could find a use for that."

"What's that queer noise?" asked Natalie.

Aileen peered through the leaves at the river. "It's only the Newgrange College boys rowing upstream," she remarked.

Everyone had to have a look then.

"They're very good," Judith pointed out. "Look how fast they're going – St Brigid's will have a job beating them."

"That's the Major's worry, not ours," replied Fidelma lazily. "There's the tea bell, thank goodness. I'm starving!"

"Come on Natalie," grinned Judith. "The boys are out of sight."

Aileen stopped them as they were leaving Barney with an imperious wave. "No talking about the party. I want it to be a surprise for Nuala. I'll tell the others too. Agreed?" She looked at all of them.

"Agreed!" came back without hesitation.

4

Mad Moments in the Museum

"Look at that necklace there, and those bracelets! Aren't they just brilliant?" cried Eithne peeping into a large display cabinet in the museum, full of gold objects.

"Fabulous and so shiny too," agreed Nuala, "though I think those twisted chains and coils are really more impressive. They're orchs. I think there's something different and original about them."

"I suppose only kings, queens and chiefs ever wore these things," Eithne said thoughtfully.

"Definitely. It makes you feel queer, doesn't it, to think that real people wore them, cleaned them and fought over them hundreds of years ago. Which reminds me – isn't it sickening the treasury room is closed today? I wanted to study the ornamentation of the chalices. I must have it right."

"It's rotten luck," replied Eithne in a sympathetic voice. "Though this part is interesting too. I loved all those wooden combs and carved animals, not to mention that sweet little leather boot."

Despite her disappointment Nuala had to agree with Eithne.

"Yes, it's been fun. I couldn't believe Sr Francis could be so pleasant. Imagine taking us to the Stephen's Green Centre for ice cream. Dublin is so hot, it was a lovely surprise."

Eithne looked at her watch. "I guess we'll be going soon."

"You're right, here's Sr Francis and she's calling to us."

They joined the first years and as they all poured through the outer area where the shop was situated Nuala remembered something she had seen on the way in. She dashed off to the shop without saying anything to Eithne who went ahead with the crowd.

"Could I have some of these postcards please, the ones with chalices on them?" she asked the woman behind the counter. She had passed the cards over to Nuala and was taking the money for them when somehow or other a pile of books which were on the counter fell over and scattered around the floor.

Nuala automatically picked up the books and passed them to the woman, who thanked her profusely. Then she set out swiftly in pursuit of Eithne and the others who had vanished out through the entrance of the museum.

She had nearly reached the outer door herself when she felt a sharp tap on her shoulder. Turning swiftly around she confronted a total stranger looking at her. Her first impression was of black wispy hair escaping from under a floppy nondescript hat, and a multicoloured scarf stuffed into a dark pink coat. Then as her arm was seized in a pincer-like grip, she became aware of large grey eyes watching her.

"Why did you do it, Miss?" asked a quiet voice. "You should know better than that."

"Know what?" Nuala was mystified.

Fixing those large eyes on Nuala again, she now clearly spoke at a slower pace, as if Nuala were half-witted. "Just put the book back and I'll say nothing this time."

Nuala, terrified, resisted the impulse to beat off the hand on her arm. Striving to speak calmly she asked, "What book? I don't know what you're talking about."

At that, the woman bent forward and seemed to pluck a book from the carrier bag in Nuala's other hand.

"This book. I saw you steal it from the shop," she said as she triumphantly waved a book in front of Nuala which she instantly recognised as one of those she had picked up from the floor of the shop only minutes before.

"I . . . I never stole that book," stammered Nuala indignantly. She looked desperately around her, but they were quite alone. Alone with a madwoman, she thought, frantically wondering should she start screaming for help.

"I won't hand you over this time if you're prepared to cooperate," was the next shock Nuala experienced.

"Cooperate? I don't understand . . . " she quavered.

"It concerns Natalia El Khadi, a pupil in your school at St Brigid's."

"I've never heard of her," Nuala said firmly. "You must have our school mixed up with another."

A crowd of chattering school children swept out of the inner room, startling the woman in pink. Nuala, feeling the iron grip relax, took her chance and pulled her arm away.

She ran out of the museum and down Kildare Street where Eithne was coming towards her, looking worried.

"Quick Eithne," Nuala shouted. "Where's the coach? There's a madwoman chasing after me."

Fortunately the school coach was parked quite near to Kildare Street and as soon as the two girls got in, Sr Francis nodded to the driver. He drove off immediately in the opposite direction. Nuala dived into her seat and hid herself from view. She was taking no chances.

As soon as the Liffey had been crossed and they were on their way to St Brigid's Nuala relaxed sufficiently to tell Eithne the whole story of her strange and frightening encounter in the museum. As they were the only third years in the party, Nuala and Eithne, sitting alone at the back of the coach, were able to talk freely without being overheard.

"She must have been mad, quite mad," remarked Eithne when she heard Nuala's tale. Shaking her head she added ghoulishly, "You were lucky to get away in one piece. You didn't notice a knife in her other hand, by any chance?"

Nuala shuddered. "I didn't see any sign of a knife" she replied thankfully, "but the way she pulled that book out of my bag couldn't have been bettered in a magic show on TV. Producing a knife wouldn't have been any trouble to that one."

Eithne decided to change the conversation, so as to take Nuala's mind off the madwoman in pink. "Can I see the cards you bought in the museum?" she asked.

"Of course," replied Nuala fishing the packet out of the carrier bag. "They are all of famous chalices," she explained to Eithne. "The top one is of the Ardagh Chalice. Look at the Celtic designs all around it, with precious stones set in the design. It says here that it was made in the tenth century." She passed over the cards to Eithne so that she could see for herself.

Eithne took her time and looked carefully at the illustrations on the cards. "Are you modelling the one in your essay on these chalices?" she asked.

"Vaguely," was the reply. "My essay starts with the silver mines. They have to burn silver first, to rid it of impurities. Then when it's refined, they have to add a certain amount of copper to make it hard enough for use as a container of any sort."

Eithne looked at Nuala with respect. "How do you know so much about silver?" she asked.

Nuala laughed ruefully "I don't know much about it at all. I just got a book from the library and read it up."

"How far have you got in your story?" asked Eithne in spite of herself.

"I've reached the part where a famous worker in silver is commissioned to make the chalice. A certain chief had a son who fell off his horse and was terribly badly injured. You can imagine how worrying it was in those days, no penicillin or drugs. The boy's parents prayed that he would get better and when he eventually did, they decided to give the local monastery church a beautiful chalice in thanksgiving for theirs son's recovery."

"What happened to the boy? Did he become famous when he grew up?" asked Eithne.

Nuala was amused. "I hadn't thought of that. It's supposed to be the chalice's story, you know. Anyway when it's finished you can read it and find out for yourself," she answered.

"I'd love to. It sounds good, not like most of them, though Gwendoline's is hilarious, like a fashion mag."

Nuala looked out the window. "We haven't far to go now. We should get back to the school in time for tea."

"Thank goodness, I'm starving. I hope you win a prize in the competition."

"I hope so too, I'm beginning to think I deserve one."

Tea was nearly over before anyone remembered to tell Nuala and Eithne the news.

"You know this Boynepeace club thing," Aileen remarked casually, "Well next Monday morning, we're going to Calfe's Pool, so that we can get to

35

know every little twig, plant and stone by their first name and we have to bring notebooks and Biros with us to write down their thoughts too."

Nuala, noticing Natalie's bored face, said mildly to her, "You never know, we might find knowing about Boyne wildlife a great help in the future."

"I'm sure it will be most useful to me," retorted Natalie in what she fancied a very sarcastic voice.

Later that night as Nuala lay in bed, Judith slipped quietly into her cubicle. "Eithne has just told me about your awful experience in the museum," she whispered.

"Oh, the woman in pink," replied Nuala. "Yes, it was quite terrifying. I don't think I'll go there again."

Judith noticed a funny look on Nuala's face. "What's the matter?" she asked anxiously.

"Nothing really, except do you think I have a mark on me that attracts weirdos? Like the sign gypsies are supposed to leave on your gate if you're a soft touch."

Judith laughed softly. "I hope not, though when you come to think of it, we have met with quite a few weirdos in the last year or so, haven't we?"

Nuala grinned in agreement as Judith left to return to her own cubicle.

5

Calfe's Pool

"It's a pity we are not nearer to the Boyne estuary," Miss Crilly confided enthusiastically to Deirdre and Ciara walking beside her as she led the Boynepeace contingent on its first outing. "They have some very interesting bird life there, including at least one sighting of a white stork, not to mention an even rarer bird, the little egret."

"I'd love to see a white stork," replied Ciara. "What could we see along the river today?"

"Lots of birds, swans, dippers and grey wagtails for instance."

"It's been so hot lately. Would that affect the wildlife?" asked Deirdre.

"I don't think it would affect the water birds, though in hot weather fishes go deeper of course. Not that that worries me," replied Miss Crilly grimly. "I disapprove of fishing and fishermen."

Not far behind the leaders, Judith was telling Aileen, Nuala and Natalie how much she appreciated the whole idea of Boynepeace. "It's lovely seeing animals in their natural surroundings, especially rare birds," she said.

"I agree it's better than being stuck in a stuffy classroom," conceded Aileen. "All the same, don't expect me to get all excited by bits of twigs and stones and about carefully entering all my findings in a notebook."

Judith laughed. "You're always the same, Aileen, pretending you're not interested in anything. I bet if we see a kingfisher today you'll just be as excited as the rest of us."

Aileen looked unconvinced.

"Did I ever tell you about the goldcrest I saw last year?" Nuala asked them. "I see I didn't. Anyway I heard a terrific thump on the sitting-room window one day at home. When I looked up I saw a tiny greenish-coloured bird sitting on the windowsill, looking very stunned. I noticed that it had a bright yellow crest shaped like a punk haircut. I couldn't believe it. After some time it recovered and flew off. I discovered it was called a goldcrest and lived in conifers. We've lots of conifers in the garden, but I never saw the goldcrest again."

Aileen looked suspiciously at Nuala. "You're not having us on, are you Nuala? Birds with punk haircuts don't sound true to me."

"Really Aileen, I wish you wouldn't accuse me of making things up, I never make things up," replied Nuala indignantly.

By this time they had reached a place near the river where Miss Crilly stopped, and gathered the class around her.

"Now girls," she announced, "the whole object of this club is to teach us respect for our

environment. That includes everything around us
– the river, the wildlife on it and around the
countryside, plant life, even the air we breathe. We
are only guardians of this planet and we should
aim to pass it on in good condition to the next
generations. Is that understood?"

A murmur of "Yes Miss Crilly" rose from the
listeners. The teacher smiled at them, then
continued briskly. "What I want you to do is to
write down anything you see of interest even if
you are not sure what the right name is. Have you
got your notebooks and Biros?"

"Yes, Miss Crilly," rose again from the girls.

"Good, now if you're not sure of the name of the
things you write down, make a little sketch and
when we get to school we can look it up and find
the correct name. Every month we'll collate all our
findings and in that way we'll soon build up a
picture of the richness of our area."

The fresh morning air had given way to a sullen
heat, so the girls really appreciated the shade of
the trees all around them.

"Do we simply record everything strange we
see?" asked Gwendoline earnestly, sporting a
beautiful leather-bound notebook.

"Anything that is unknown to you," replied the
teacher, secretly wondering what extraordinary
objects would turn up in Gwendoline's notebook.
She looked around impatiently, consulting her
watch. "I thought Mr Greene and the Newgrange
boys would be here long ago," she muttered
crossly. "The rendezvous was arranged for ten-

thirty AM, and it's ten-fifty already."

Five minutes later she spoke again. "They mustn't be coming. I'm taking you to Calfe's Pool. It isn't far from here. I know kingfishers are nesting there, and if we wait very very quietly for a while there's a good chance of seeing one, but we do have to be very quiet."

She led the way followed by the girls who were terribly excited at the thought of seeing a kingfisher. Even Natalie felt a stirring of interest. A kingfisher she thought would be something worth seeing.

It didn't take long to reach Calfe's Pool, which had been formed by the bank of the river curving inland for about a hundred yards and then curving out again, thus causing quite a sizeable water catchment between the two banks.

They had passed through a heavily-wooded area to get to the pool whose banks were covered thickly with undergrowth. The girls dispersed themselves around this, sitting down cautiously and peering through leaves and branches so as not to miss anything that might pass by. Miss Crilly checked everyone's position, making sure no one was too near the water – she didn't want anyone falling in. Then she spoke in a low voice.

"The nest is in the riverbank further along. I don't want to go too near, for fear of disturbing the chicks."

It was very peaceful in the cool dim light of the undergrowth. Gwendoline whispered to Monica: "I hope nothing crawls into my jeans, but if it does

I'll be ready to record it," and she slid her hand into her pocket and furtively withdrew the leather notebook.

This remark made Monica so uneasy that she concentrated on watching the ground for any signs of creepy-crawlies, quite forgetting the kingfisher in consequence.

Most of the watchers felt quite sleepy. Nuala, leaning comfortably against the trunk of a tree, started thinking about her essay, mentally rewriting several pages of it and choosing new names for various characters. Beside her Aileen, planning the details of Nuala's surprise party, wondered for the hundredth time how she could possibly make a birthday cake for Nuala in school and so win her bet against the others.

The minutes passed by slowly. Just when the watchers felt that they had waited long enough to allay the fears of even the fussiest kingfisher, Judith, who was one of the nearest to the river, noticed the arrival of a small bird. Her excitement mounted when she saw that its shoulders and wings were a turquoise blue. She nudged Josie and pointed silently. Soon word spread around. The bird flew over and perched on a dead branch which must have fallen from a tree up river and, drifting down, got jammed against the bank in front of the hidden girls. As they watched, the bird dived into the river, returning almost immediately with quite a sizeable fish caught in its long black pointed beak. A ripple of agitation passed through the watchers as the long-awaited kingfisher efficiently bashed the hapless fish against the branch before swallowing it head first. After its lunch the kingfisher preened lightly, then gazed at its reflection in the smooth river below.

Everyone was almost afraid to breathe for fear of disturbing this entrancing spectacle, though Gwendoline furtively opened her notebook ready for action.

Suddenly the sound of tramping feet and boys' voices broke the silence. There was a flash of blue flying swiftly over the river and out of sight. The newcomers had startled the kingfisher away.

The girls stood and glared out of the undergrowth at a stockily-built man who was standing there, looking with interest around him. Within minutes groups of boys, in twos and threes, arrived on the scene and joined them.

Aileen heard Natalie draw in her breath and murmur in a surprised voice, "Boys out here."

Gwendoline consulted her watch and wrote carefully in her notebook: "Eleven fifteen. Kingfisher sighted eating lunch. Eleven twenty. Boys sighted. Probably Newgrange College." Miss Crilly had told them to record anything strange, she argued to herself, and boys in the area certainly came under this heading.

"Mr Greene," stormed Miss Crilly. "Do you realise that you are thirty minutes late, not to mention frightening away our kingfisher?"

Mr Greene wasn't the slightest bit upset by her tone. "We were delayed by a false sighting of what we thought was a peregrine falcon," he explained calmly. "We are here now, so no harm's done."

Everyone watched with interest as Miss Crilly's face got redder and redder but just as the young onlookers thought that they were going to witness something special in rows, Miss Crilly composed herself.

"Girls!" she ordered. "Go down at once to the road and wait for me there. I have something private I wish to say to Mr Greene."

While the two teachers withdrew themselves further away from the river, the girls wandered down to the road where they fraternised with the boys, some of whom they knew already.

Judith was describing the first sight of the kingfisher to Nuala, Aileen and Natalie when they were interrupted by a voice saying, "Hi Aileen. What's the crack?"

When Aileen turned around she was surprised to see her cousin David and another boy standing there.

"Hi David," she replied. "This is a surprise. I didn't realise that you cared for the environment."

David laughed. "You don't think I had any choice in the matter, do you? Have sense, Aileen. Meet Paul, Paul – Aileen."

"Hi Paul, this is Nuala and Judith, you met them already, David, and Natalie who's new this term."

"What's Mr Greene like?" asked Nuala, curious to find out more about Bill's best man.

"He's all right but a bit mad," replied David casually.

"He's not a bit mad, he's crackers, completely

43

crackers," burst out Paul in his deep voice. "You won't believe this but he's building a car out of waste paper and *Jungle* cans."

"You must be joking," laughed Aileen. "We're not idiots, you know. Nobody can make a car out of waste paper."

"Anyway," protested Nuala, "surely he's against cars, all that petrol and those fumes. What about the ozone layer?"

"You don't think he'll be using fossil fuels, do you?" replied David briskly. "These girls know nothing, Paul. The Greene superauto will be run by solar energy – that's power from the sun, in case you don't understand the scientific term," he added patronizingly.

Aileen gave him a withering look but refrained from rising to the bait.

Josie joined them. "Hi David," she greeted him warmly. "They're just messing aren't they, when they say Mr Greene keeps a huge plastic vat of wet wastepaper in his bedroom?"

The two boys laughed rudely.

"Not his bedroom, a special outhouse," David replied. "He's working on a secret formula that will turn it into a material as strong as steel."

"That's not the important thing in his life though. What he would really like us all to do is go back to the simple life that our ancestors led. Eat nuts, fish and berries. Wear animal skins," Paul informed them.

"No wonder Miss Crilly dislikes him. She's a smart dresser," stated Aileen firmly. "And I know

44

for a fact she hates fishermen. She finds fishing a cruel sport."

"There's nothing cruel about fishing, it requires a great deal of skill," Paul retorted hotly. "I wouldn't mind if we had fishing instead of class."

"Ugh!" shuddered Natalie. "Smelly skins to wear and no hot water or shops. The simple life would not suit me at all."

David and Paul were highly amused by her distaste.

Nuala had been thinking about Mr Greene's ideas of life. "Some of our ancestors didn't live such a simple life, judging from all those gold things in the museum," she said. "Kings and chiefs had slaves to cook for them, heat water, wash their clothes, etc. Think of how important this part of the county was in ancient times. I wouldn't be surprised if there was lots of gold and silver treasure buried in the ground around here, maybe just where we're standing."

"I wouldn't mind finding a few gold bracelets or one of those gold neck things," agreed Paul. "Then I could buy a brilliant computer with the money, one which responds to voice commands."

"What would you command it to do?" asked Natalie.

"Maths. I would lie back and let it get everything right," he replied.

This was greeted with laughter, some of it derisive.

"What we need is a metal detector," said Aileen. "Then when all the Boynepeacers are enthusing

45

over plants and animals, the rest of us could be going carefully over the ground and sussing out the gold treasure."

"Whereupon the two boys could steal out of Newgrange College at night and dig up the gold for us," suggested Nuala. "We could give them a portion of the reward of course. Ten per cent would be generous, don't you think, girls?"

The two boys didn't join in the chorus of approval which greeted her words. "I thought girls wanted an equal share of the workload nowadays," remarked David.

"So we do. There's acres of ground here and detecting the stuff would be the really hard work," retorted Aileen swiftly.

"There's something in the idea all the same," said Paul. "Nobody has dug around this place for centuries, there could be treasure here. Maybe you should give it a try." He looked at Nuala and Aileen as he spoke.

David laughed scornfully. "You must be joking, Paul. Girls finding treasure? They wouldn't know how to start going about it."

"What do you mean, David?" Aileen screeched at him. "The cheek of that. Girls can do anything boys can."

"All right. Keep your hair on. Paul and I will hide something, and we'll challenge you to find it."

Nuala was amused. "You need to do better than that. After all, you could hide it almost anywhere."

"I know," replied Paul. "We'll work out something with proper instructions and clues. It'll

46

be something new to do anyway.

"If we do that," David asked Nuala, Judith and Aileen, "will you accept the challenge?"

"Work it out and send it to us," Nuala replied, "and if it's well done, we'll show you how good we are."

"Yes," agreed Aileen. "It's up to you."

Just then Mr Greene arrived down at the road and called the boys to order. It was time for both parties to return to their respective schools. So David and Paul said goodbye and went off after Mr Greene.

That night as they were going up the stairs to bed, a preoccupied Aileen rushed out past Nuala and Judith without saying a word to either of them.

"What's up with Aileen?" asked Judith.

"I don't know. I hope it's nothing serious," replied Nuala. "All I know is every time I've seen her since we got back from Calfe's Pool, she's been buried in a cookery book."

6

Aileen Accepts a Challenge

"Is Nuala here?" asked an anxious voice, as Aileen's head appeared among the fresh green leaves of the giant beech, where Judith and Josie were relaxing with Eithne and Fidelma during the free period which they always had at the end of afternoon school.

Judith looked lazily down at the newcomer.

"'Fraid not," she replied in a faraway voice. "She has gone off with Natalie to play tennis. Where they get the energy from in this hot weather beats me."

"Great!" was Aileen's surprising response, as she climbed nimbly up the tree, hauling a bulky blue plastic bag behind her. Under the fascinated gaze of her friends, she settled herself comfortably on the branch next to Judith's, sighing with relief. Opening the blue bag she produced from its interior a large book with *Almost Instant* inscribed in clear gold letters on its white front cover. Under the inscription could be seen in smaller writing *50 Easy Ways to Cake Making*.

"I want your advice on which of these cakes I

should make for Nuala's surprise party," Aileen requested in a businesslike way as she turned the pages of the book.

"You're not going ahead with that crazy plan?" Josie asked scornfully. "It's impossible. For instance, you need eggs and butter for most cakes and either a mixer or food processor to do the mixing, and how on earth could you cook it?"

Aileen, who had relaxed, stiffened. "Josie, when I say I'm making a cake for Nuala, I mean I'm making a cake for her," she retorted proudly. "And nobody, but nobody is putting me off."

"Have it your own way," Josie shrugged her shoulders. "If you want to make an idiot of yourself, go ahead. Don't blame me when people like Natalie Frossart laugh at you. You've never made a cake in your life, have you?"

Aileen was so incensed by this tactless remark that she slammed *Almost Instant* closed with a snap, and made as if to leave, her eyes flashing with anger.

Judith hastened to appease the would-be confectioner. She placed a restraining hand on Aileen's arm and pleaded, "Don't go, it's this awful heat, it's affected her brain. Read out a few names and we'll help you to choose."

Josie made a funny noise in her throat, and looked pointedly down at the river, as if she wished to disassociate herself from the whole party.

"Do Aileen," urged Eithne, good-naturedly supporting her cousin's efforts to keep the peace.

"Very well," agreed Aileen a little coldly, opening the book again and slowly turning the pages. "Here's an Almond and Honey Twist or Paddy's Chocolate Ring . . . " She murmured the list of ingredients to herself and hastily passed on to the next chapter. "What do you think of Coffee Butter Cake, or Strawberry Split or even Lemon Cream Walnut Cake?"

"They all sound yummy. Read on," ordered Judith closing her eyes. The heat was making her sleepy.

"Let me see, Gingerbread Ring . . . Chocolate Layer Cake . . . " replied Aileen warming to her subject. "Austrian Gateau . . . Whole Cherry Cake . . . " Her voice trailed off as she wondered why the book was called *Easy Ways to Cake Making* – they all seemed very difficult to her. Josie was right, she thought, the cake idea is silly. Then her eye caught a recipe at the bottom of the page. It was a lemon cheesecake made with biscuit crumbs, melted butter, cream cheese, a lemon, and a packet of lemon jelly.

"Don't read any more," implored Fidelma. "You're making my mouth water. I could just see that Strawberry Split. It's sheer torture."

Aileen laughed triumphantly. "I don't need to. I've just found one." Popping the book back in her bag, she slid off the branch and down the tree making a lot of noise in her haste.

Judith's eyes flew open. "What is it, Aileen?" she asked, while even Josie turned away from her contemplation of the river.

"Wait and see. Have your fifty pence ready, Josie," floated up to them. Then she was gone. There was a silence for a while after she left.

"What do you think of this midnight party, Eithne?" asked Josie mildly. She seemed to have recovered her good humour. "You weren't here when Natalie thought it up."

"I think it could be fabulous on the castle roof, cool and mysterious in this awful heat," was Eithne's reply.

"I haven't slept much these last few nights myself," agreed Josie. "It will be a nice change from the stuffy dorm."

"It'll be brilliant fun," said Judith. "As long as we're not caught, of course."

"We'll just have to be extra careful," Fidelma pointed out. "I've never been to the roof. I believe the view from it is wonderful."

"Someone is coming!" warned Josie. She peered down through the branches. "It's only Nuala. I wonder what she did with Natalie?"

It wasn't long before Nuala joined them.

"Hi chucks," she called cheerfully. "Anyone for a nice cool drink?" Before they had time to answer she had handed a can of *Jungle* to each of them.

"Oh brilliant, Nuala," gasped Josie. "Just what we were all dying for."

Judith pressed back the ring on her can. "Thanks, Nuala. Where did you find these?"

Nuala took a long drink. "Aaah! That's better." She looked at Judith. "Where did I get them from? You wouldn't believe it but I caught the tuck shop open. So I dashed in and bought a few things there before it folded its tent and slipped quietly away again."

The others laughed.

"You were lucky. It hasn't been open for at least a week," grinned Judith.

"It's those fifth years," Josie explained. "Since Sharon Kennedy and her pals were given charge of it, it only opens when they're in the mood."

"True," agreed Eithne. "What did you do with Natalie, Nuala?"

"Natalie was beating me hollow at tennis, when fate in the shape of Monica came up and said Gobnait was looking for her. Natalie just gave a shriek and dashed off without a backward glance. I was never so glad of anything in my life. It's too hot for tennis."

"It's never too hot for Natalie," suggested Josie. "I know she comes from Scotland but I'd never have guessed she was Scottish."

Judith shook her head. "She isn't Scottish," she pronounced. "She can't be. With her colouring and that accent she must be from Southern France or Italy or possibly North Africa. She is very mysterious about it, all the same, isn't she?"

"She is," agreed Fidelma. "Someone, Ciara, I think, or Gwendoline, asked her where she was from and she shut up and walked away."

"Well, I suppose it's her own business," said Josie thoughtfully. "Her parents might be divorced and she doesn't want to talk about it. Something like that – you can't blame her."

"The weirdest thing happened to me in the tuck shop," said Nuala, dismissing Natalie from their minds. "When I went in there to get the *Jungle*, I saw Aileen buying biscuits and asking for butter and a lemon of all things. Needless to say they didn't stock either of them. Then Aileen pretended not to know me. Just looked through me and ran out the door of the shop. I wonder why . . . "

"It must be this awful heat," Judith broke in desperately. "It's affected her mind. I thought she was looking very queer myself today."

"Absolutely," agreed Josie with relish. "You should have seen the wild way she answered me only a while ago when I begged her to give up a crazy plan she had in mind."

Nuala looked disgusted. "Are you two crazy or something?" she protested. "I know the weather is the hottest it's been in years, but it's not *that* hot. There's nothing wrong with Aileen's mind, she's just up to something. I suppose if I were to tell you that Gwendoline and Deirdre are going around collecting glass jars, you'd say it was the heat too."

Eithne's voice broke the rather strained silence. "How much do I owe you for that can of *Jungle*, Nuala?" she asked.

"Oh nothing at all. My godmother sent me a very generous present of money, this morning." She brushed aside their thanks with, "Think nothing of it, it was a pleasure."

"Were you serious, Nuala, about looking for treasure around the Boyne?" asked Josie.

"Why not?" replied Nuala. "There must be some

gold or precious metals lying around. Think of all the years the kings lived at Tara. As we all know, the Tara brooch was found by children at Bettystown, and that's not that far from here."

"We'll need a metal detector," Judith said briskly. "There's no way we could look over a big place like this otherwise. Where do we get one?"

They all looked blankly at her.

"I haven't a clue," confessed Nuala. "Somehow I don't think the village shop keeps them."

"Well, I like that," said Josie. "First of all you get us all excited about finding priceless treasure, and when all we want is a little thing like a metal detector you don't know where to get one."

"I'm sorry, Josie, all I can say is I'll ask Sr Gobnait. My mother told me that Sr Gobnait once told her that she could take care of anything."

Judith grinned. "I don't think your mother meant that sort of thing," she pointed out.

"Don't be a pig, Nuala, you know if you ask Gobnait she'll either take over or forbid it," protested Josie.

"I think I hear the bell. We'd better go," said Fidelma.

"Don't worry, Josie. I'll spend most of study thinking of a way of getting Gobnait to give me the info without realising what I'm up to," Nuala promised as they climbed down Barney and started walking back to the castle.

7

Nuala's Midnight Party

The school clock had hardly struck two AM when the strident clamour of Aileen's alarm going off under her pillow woke her up. Automatically her hand reached out and switched it off. Then as remembrance flooded her mind she jumped out of bed and quietly flitted around the dormitory calling the others to get up.

Within minutes the sound of creaks, bumps and smothered giggles could be heard, followed shortly by a number of figures weighed down with bags, leaving the dormitory.

Judith carefully closed the door behind the last of these. Then she counted to one hundred slowly, and went into Nuala's cubicle and gently shook her. "Nuala, wake up, Nuala," she urged in a low voice. "Wake up."

Nuala opened her eyes and stared uncomprehendingly at her. "What's the matter?" she asked sleepily.

"Nothing," Judith hissed back. "But you've got to get up at once."

Nuala sat up, yawned and rubbed her eyes.

"Why do I have to get up. Is the school on fire or something?"

Judith laughed quietly. "No, nothing like that," she reassured her, "but we do have to assemble on the castle roof."

Nuala looked at her in amazement. "The castle roof. Why the castle roof?" she asked as she swung herself out of bed and shuffled her slippers on. "Has Gobnait gone crackers? We're not even allowed on the castle roof," she muttered as she put on the dressing-gown, which Judith had thoughtfully handed to her.

Judith hustled her out of the dormitory and along the dimly-lit corridors.

"Where's everybody?" Nuala asked as they hurried up a flight of stairs, and along another corridor.

"They are all up there, waiting for us," was Judith's firm response.

It didn't take long to reach the enclosed staircase which led to the roof of the castle. Judith pushed Nuala through the door, locking it behind them and pocketing the key. When they reached the top of the staircase, they found it opened on to a large porch-like building whose sides were glazed with thick glass. As Judith and Nuala passed through the door of this building the heat hit them like a blast from a furnace.

"Gosh, look at the height of the walls here!" commented Nuala. "No wonder it's so hot."

"And so dark. I can't see a thing," agreed Judith.

The darkness was suddenly pierced by a row of lights which moved silently towards the pair of them. As they watched the lights formed a semicircle around them.

"Happy birthday, Nuala!" broke the silence.

"Happy birthday, Nuala." It sounded like Aileen's voice.

"Surprise, surprise! Happy birthday, Nuala!" chorused other voices. Then a dumbfounded Nuala realised that the lights were really candles stuck in jamjars and the voices belonged to the girls of St Ita's dormitory. They all surrounded Nuala and congratulated her, clapping noisily.

"Thank you, thank you," she stammered. "I never guessed a thing, truly I didn't. I just thought it was some mad thing of Sr Gobnait's."

Aileen led Nuala across the roof to where a chimney stack abutted against one of the walls forming a sheltered space. Here a table of sorts had been set up with crisps, peanuts, popcorn, chocolates and other good things attractively laid out on it. Aileen placed the candle in its jar in the centre of the table.

"It's really two benches pushed together," she explained proudly to Nuala, "with one of my sheets for a table-cloth, but doesn't it look yummy?"

"Brilliant!" was Nuala's reaction. "I don't know what to say except thank you again."

Aileen suddenly darted off returning shortly with a cake of uneven shape which wobbled slightly. Chocolate flakes surrounded the three birthday candles on it. They flickered bravely in the darkness. "The birthday cake as promised," she announced. "Made on the premises. I will collect the fifty pences later," and she placed the cake beside the candle in the middle of the table.

"You really made it after all," exclaimed Josie. "I don't believe it. How did you manage it, Aileen?"

Aileen looked proudly at her. "It would take too long to relate the difficulties involved in producing this cake, suffice it to say that they were terrible, but I overcame them," she replied loftily, thereby glossing over the fact that the cake was mostly made with cream cheese and a packet of lemon jelly, and that Sr Rosario had very kindly given her refrigerator space in the kitchen, without a murmur.

Josie, who knew nothing of this, was visibly impressed and agreed to pay up first thing in the morning, which put Aileen in the best of humour.

In consequence not a shadow lay across the feast when the ten of them sat down, Nuala in the place of honour. At Aileen's suggestion they had taken off their dressing-gowns and used them as cushions against the hard dusty floor of the roof, which caused some difficulties the next morning for those who had picked delicate pastel shades for the aforementioned garments.

When everything had been eaten, Nuala blew out the candles on the cake, and Aileen served out portions of it.

"It's yummy," pronounced the grateful birthday girl, "but why three candles?"

"I only had three," replied Aileen. "It's the spirit that counts."

"I just thought that you were being tactful, but

the cake is delicious and very suitable in the heat," declared Nuala.

When everything had been cleared away and thrown into the black plastic bags which had been used to bring up the goods originally, Eithne said, "It's amazing, it took three bags to bring up the stuff and only two to take it away," while Aileen nudged Judith and whispered about the present.

"A present, as well as a party and there's tomorrow too," pronounced Nuala gratefully. "I hope I have a birthday like this every year."

Judith produced a small flat box and solemnly handed it to Nuala. "I present this birthday gift to you, Nuala, from the whole of St Ita's dorm, and may you have many happy years of wearing it."

Nuala tore off the wrapping, crying, "Oh, a vox watch! I've always wanted one. How does it work?"

"It's a watch that tells you the time, you press this little bar here, and listen," said Aileen taking the watch from Nuala. "It is now two-thirty AM" said a pleasant male voice.

"It's weird, isn't it? Especially with all the darkness around," cried Josie. "I always feel like saying 'Thank you Mr . . . ' when I hear the voice."

"You can use it like a stop-watch and it plays Bach to wake you up, if you set the alarm," explained Aileen. "Isn't it brill?"

"I can't think of anything to say again which would surprise my family, but it's true. You're brilliant friends, thank you for this beautiful watch and the party too," said Nuala who was really overcome by it all.

"Sit down everyone," ordered Aileen who was enjoying herself immensely. "Miss E Murray has been persuaded to entertain us with a story about Collier the Robber."

They moved over to the benches which were back in their rightful place once again. Nobody used them, however, as with one accord the whole group sat on the ground with their backs against the warm wall.

Aileen placed all the candles in a little circle in front of them. They cast a feeble glow which seemed to increase the vast expanse of darkness around them.

"Michael Collier, the highwayman, was born over two hundred years ago," began Eithne, who knew not only Natalie but Monica, Gwendoline and Deirdre would hardly have heard of him. "He was a sort of Irish Robin Hood, stealing from the rich and generous to the poor. There are loads of stories about him, but the one I'm going to tell you is the most famous one."

Eithne's voice sounded a bit eerie in the darkness. It made the story more interesting, but they all moved closer together just the same.

"Though Collier stole quite a lot of money, he didn't keep it for long. Apart from the fact that he was generous to the poor, he was also careless with money himself. During one bad winter when few travelled the roads, he became very short of cash. In desperation he decided to rob the mail coach which travelled from Dublin to Belfast. He knew that it was a very dangerous thing to take on, first the guard was armed with a sword and a blunderbuss, but also the male passengers would be carrying pistols. Then as it was the royal mail, he'd have the authorities chasing after him too. However, he had outwitted the military many times before and it was well worth the chance. He laid his plans and spent the next few days going around collecting old hats and coats."

"Did he ride a horse?" Natalie wanted to know. "Like the highwaymen we read about in books?"

"No," replied Eithne. "They say that with the aid of a long ash pole, he could outrun any soldiers who were on horses chasing him. Anyway, to get back to the story. On the fateful night in question when the mail coach complete with passengers left Princes Street in Dublin, the GPO hadn't been built then, it was snowing hard. As the heavy coach lumbered along in the darkness, the driver must have dreaded the long journey in the freezing weather. Think how hard it was on the poor horses. Maybe the guard hoped it would keep robbers at home too.

"In those days the road between Drumcondra and Santry was feared by travellers, as robbery was so common. The highwaymen used to hide in the numerous woods in this area, one was even reputed to live in a hollow tree near Santry, just popping out when he wanted to hold anyone up.

"Collier arrived at a place called Bloody Hollow on the way to Swords and arranged some old coats and hats which he had collected on a hedge at the side of a steep road, rising out of the hollow.

"Soon enough the coach appeared driven at speed through Bloody Hollow. This is the story the driver told the sheriff afterwards. 'It was like this, sir. All the way from Sackville Street, it was snowing hard. By the time we got to Bloody Hollow the poor horses were in a lather. The darkness was setting in too. As we climbed slowly up the slope after the Hollow, this huge man suddenly leaped out into the middle of the road, barring the way. I pulled the coach to stop, and then I heard him shout over at the ditch. 'Don't fire until I give the command!' We looked over and though the light was very poor, we could see a bunch of desperate characters peering over the hedge at us. At that the villain in the road called, 'Now, gentlemen, resistance is useless. My men line the ditches. They only want a word from me and they'll riddle the lot of you.' Looking at the size of him and his treacherous black villainy, I could well believe they would. I was mighty afeared but I hesitated to give in all the same. The blackguard must have guessed for then he shouted in a loud commanding voice, 'Steady boys, cover them well, horses and all.' The passengers by this time were hanging out the windows. When they heard this order, they got out and handed over all their valuables and money. He had a good haul, I must say. Then the cheeky devil stepped to one side of the road and waved me on, calling as we passed, 'A safe journey to you!'

"Next morning when a squad of Dragoons galloped out from Dublin to investigate the incident, they found six sets of hats and coats arranged on a hedge in Bloody Hollow. But Collier was miles and miles away by this time laughing all the way." Eithne finished her story to laughter and clapping.

"That was really clever of him, wasn't it?" Nuala said after the clapping had died down. "We must try it out sometime."

"We must," agreed Judith followed by a few sleepy assents from the others.

Deirdre broke the silence. "I never remember such a hot night," she commented in a drowsy voice.

Aileen looked around. "Do you want to go back to bed?" she asked impatiently. "You all sound half asleep."

No one wanted to go back to the dorm, they were all too comfortable.

"What about a ghost story?" suggested Natalie. "That'll keep us awake."

"Nuala, it's your turn," said Judith.

"Come on, Nuala, sing for your supper!" called the others.

8

The Storm Breaks

"As it happens, I could tell you a story which would chill the very blood in your veins, and drive the pretty colour from your cheeks," said Nuala dramatically.

Aileen was unimpressed. "Tell your story then. It's so hot tonight, I'd love to have my blood chilled."

Even though it was still dark it was indeed unusually warm and close, especially for that time of night.

"Just look at those candles, I've never seen such perfectly shaped flames, not a flicker or quiver in them," Nuala pointed out, reverting to her usual voice. "It's so still, as if it were waiting for something to happen."

"Just like us, waiting for your story," chipped in Josie.

"You won't be so keen when I tell you that my story concerns one Thelma McDonagh – you remember her, don't you Aileen?" replied Nuala pinching Aileen's arm significantly.

"Oh, that one!" cried Aileen, mystified but loyal as always. She had never even heard the name before. "I remember her well."

"Well may you call her 'that one'. She was in fifth year, a well-built bossy know-all, something like Sharon Kennedy. One night she got lost in St Brigid's and saw something so horrible, weird and monstrous, that her face changed and it never looked right again."

"So that's what happened to old Thelma then," interrupted Aileen cheekily. "I've often wondered why she was so odd-looking. Her face had kind of slipped to one side."

"Shush, let Nuala tell us the story," complained Monica impatiently.

"Shut up, Aileen!" came from Eithne and Fidelma.

Nuala calmly ignored these interruptions. She took up her tale again. "Of course you all know the big door near that long window, just beyond Sr Imelda's room, with strange signs marked on it and always locked. Anyway one night Thelma couldn't get to sleep – by the way it's just a coincidence, of course, but she slept in our dormitory, near the front window. Where you sleep, Deirdre, I think."

"It doesn't matter where she slept. What happened to her is what we want to know," exclaimed Gwendoline.

"What an impatient lot you are! Thelma was a bit like that too. She tossed and turned for hours and then she remembered a bar of rum-and-raisin chocolate which she had left in the common room. She tried not to think about it, but every time she was about to slip into sleep, she would suddenly see this monster bar in its dark brown cover, even taste its beautiful flavour for a second, and then she would jerk fully awake. At last she decided the only thing to do was to go down to the common room, and get it.

"At first all went well, she managed to reach the common room, found the chocolate and ate it. Then, fortified for the return journey, she crept up the dormitory stairs again. It was very quiet and very, very dark. Despite the chocolate she felt nervous, and jumped at every creak of the ancient staircase which generations of schoolgirls had worn smooth. A further shock awaited her when she reached the dormitories. Someone must have switched off the usual low lights in the corridors. Panic set in, as she wandered up and down hopelessly lost. Then she noticed a warm glow coming from a door somewhere near the end of a passage. She hastened forward, her heart beating with relief.

"As she was about to reach the door where the light was coming from, she heard something like this . . . " Nuala leaned forward and rapped the nearest wooden bench three times sharply. The unexpected sound made them all jump and two candles were knocked over.

"Oh God," quavered Monica who was inclined to be nervous.

"The door opened slowly" said Nuala. "She heard a terrible crash and then she saw the most horrible . . . "

What Thelma saw was never revealed for at that

moment an ear-splitting peal of thunder crashed directly above the castle, followed minutes later by a flash of jagged lightning. All the candles flickered and went out leaving the party-goers in complete darkness.

They were too stunned to do anything but scream for the first few minutes. Then they scrambled to put on their dressing-gowns and tried to make their way to the porch. Though they were terrified by the crashing thunder and the forked lightning, at least they could see where to go. Soon they safely reached the glazed porch. Aileen, by some miracle, had managed to grab the matches and a candle.

"Thank goodness you made us tidy up after the meal, Aileen," said Nuala. "We'll wait for the next flash, then Josie, Aileen and I will rush over and pick up the bags."

They hadn't long to wait. The flashes were coming in quick succession. After a few false starts they were successful in getting away and soon they returned panting, with all the bags. Aileen lit the candle and triumphantly the ten revellers went down the staircase only to find that the door at the base was securely locked.

Judith put her hands up to her face. "I must have lost the key," she wailed. "I know I put it in the pocket of my dressing-gown."

"What'll we do?" asked Monica fearfully.

"We'll have to find it, that's all," replied Nuala cheerfully, leading the way upstairs again. Somehow nobody felt like braving the elements.

As they stood silently watching the lightning and listening to the thunder, they were startled by a man's voice saying "It is three-thirty AM."

Monica jumped and grabbed Judith's arm. "It's only Nuala's vox watch," explained Judith, rubbing the afflicted part. It wasn't the first time that someone had grabbed her arm that night.

"The thunder is moving away," said Eithne. "I think we should tie all our belts together and push them through one of those slits in the wall, and try and contact one of the dorms below us."

"Do you mean climb down like Tarzan?" asked Natalie in a worried voice.

Eithne laughed. "No, we'll have to tie something on the very end of our belts so that it will tap against a window."

"We might as well try that as anything," agreed Josie. "I hope they aren't heavy sleepers."

Nobody really thought it would work, but it was better than doing nothing. So they all gave up their dressing-gown belts and Eithne and Fidelma knotted them carefully, then they tied a few empty *Jungle* cans to one end.

The thunder was only really grumbling above them now, so the party set forth bravely and pushed the improvised rope through one of the apertures in the wall. Eithne and Fidelma rattled the cans and waved the rope in and out vigorously, unaware that the window they had selected as St Catherine's dormitory was really Sr Gobnait's bedroom.

"It's getting light, I can see things," said Nuala, yawning hugely. "We've tried long enough, pull it up again."

Just then Judith gave a screech of joy. "Nuala, I see it, it's under that bench, the key I mean."

So the twins pulled up the belts.

A minute later Sr Gobnait sat up in bed. Wondering what had woken her, she put out her hand and switched on her light, only to discover that the storm had fused the lights. She got out of bed, and picked up a small torch. Slipping into her dressing-gown she set off to switch on the emergency generator.

Nuala and Judith had just checked that they had left nothing behind them on the roof when the rain came pelting down. Once again they all trooped down the staircase but this time they successfully got through the door only to find the school was in total darkness.

Luckily, Aileen had matches in her pocket and with their help, Nuala rooting through the various bags managed to find a candle. She lit it and holding it up high, whispered to everyone to follow her closely.

They set off with Monica and Gwendoline taking the rear. All went well until they came to a corner, where Gwendoline slipped and bumped into Monica. In the subsequent confusion Monica and Gwendoline unwittingly took the wrong turn.

"There they are ahead, look!" said Gwendoline.

"Let's hurry and catch up with them," replied Monica nervously. "I know it's been all great fun, but I wish I was back in my bed."

They hurried as fast as they could, and were

almost at the place where they could see a glow of light, when they heard three distinct loud knocks, followed by a crash, and a door opened quietly almost in front of them.

As they watched in horror a huge shadow, grotesque and awful, loomed up before them. Without a sound they turned and ran back down the way they came, not heeding where they were going and turned the corner. Suddenly the lights came on in the corridors, and still not saying a word, the two girls kept running until they reached St Ita's dormitory and threw themselves into their respective beds and pulled the bedclothes over their heads.

Up in the corridor which Monica and Gwendoline had so recently vacated, Sr Gobnait came of the room where the emergency generator was housed looking dusty but satisfied.

"I must get Bradley up here tomorrow," she muttered to herself. "That switch was very stiff."

The following evening Natalie walked over to where Gwendoline and Monica were sitting huddled together on one of the common room couches.

"I want to ask you two just one question," she said in her frank way. "Why do you keep looking at yourselves in that mirror all day and then muttering about it?"

Gwendoline pushed the mirror deeply down the side of the couch and out of sight.

"What mirror?" she asked. "Really Natalie, you have the funniest fantasies, hasn't she, Monica?"

"Absolutely Gwendoline, I hope it's not catching."

9

Rain and Races

"Ever since that storm on the night of your party Nuala, the weather has been cooler and wetter," remarked Judith. "Just look at that rain." She turned away from the classroom window, and looked at Nuala who was writing as if her life depended on it.

"It's after four, Nuala, and everyone left ages ago. I don't believe you've heard a word I've said."

Nuala looked up. "I certainly did. The weather is back to normal, cool and wet, and everyone has gone to do exercises in the gym instead of tennis," she replied as if she had learned it all off.

Judith had to laugh as she sat down in the desk beside hers. "How is the canticle going?" she asked, referring to Nuala's entry for the history competition.

"Not too bad, I think," Nuala answered.

"Where have you got to?" Judith was interested.

"Well as you know the chalice was made in thanksgiving for little Feargal's life being spared. The monastery had quite a few chalices but nothing as beautiful or as precious as my one.

71

Every time they had any special ceremonies, it would always be taken out and used. One dreadful day many years later, the monastery was attacked by Vikings and all the monks killed. Of course they looted all the valuable altar vessels then, including the precious chalice. However, as they left, they were pursued and overtaken by people from the area. A battle took place, the man who had the chalice got away, but he was so badly wounded that in his flight he never noticed that he had dropped it. It fell into a hole in the ground where it lay hidden for centuries. Of course, that's only the storyline. I hope I've written it better than that."

"It sounds as if you are near the end. Most people are still struggling with the early part. I know I am," replied Judith.

"I want to get it finished. I'm not sure who'll find the chalice though, I haven't decided yet."

"I suppose it will have to end up in a museum," suggested Judith.

"I'm not sure about that either. I feel chalices should go to churches, after all that's what they were made for," replied Nuala, frowning as she spoke.

"Miss Ryan says it's too dangerous for the churches. No security. People would steal priceless things like that from them," Judith informed her. "It would cost thousands to insure your chalice."

"I suppose so. Let's go down and join the others," suggested Nuala.

The door opened and Josie came in. "So that's

where you are!" she cried excitedly. "Come on down to the common room. Exercises in the gym were cancelled. We're watching racing from Punchestown and Gwendoline is taking bets on the next race."

Nuala and Judith were astonished at her news.

"I can't believe it, Gwendoline taking bets! What happened to her?" asked Judith.

Josie threw her long bushy hair back from her face. "I don't know," she replied. "I think it might have been the sight of her mother on the members' stand which reminded her that she knew the owner of Mr Pickles, the favourite."

"Let's go down at once," suggested Nuala, asking Josie in a business-like way, "What's the price?"

"Fifty pence," grinned Josie. "The winnings will be good as the whole year is there and they're all placing bets."

Nuala jumped the last few steps of the stairs, landing with a thump on the polished floor. Luckily for her, Sr Gobnait wasn't around. "Where's Aileen?" she asked. "I haven't seen her since she went off to answer the phone."

"She's in the parlour with her mother," replied Josie.

The common room was in an uproar of excitement. Gwendoline had commandeered the table and was busily writing down bets in her science copy. Monica, sitting on her right, was simultaneously tearing up strips of paper for tickets and calling out the names of the runners. "Bootpolish, Twilight, Pink Carnation, High Flyer,

Dark Beauty, Pride of Blackrock, Belladonna and Mr Pickles who is the favourite."

Nuala and Judith pushed their way through the excited crowd.

"Bootpolish!" called Nuala without hesitation, placing a fifty pence coin on the table.

Gwendoline carefully filled in the details in her copy book, marked one of the strips of paper and handed it to Nuala. "Your ticket," she informed her. "Next please," she called briskly.

"Why Gwendoline, I never knew you had bookie blood in you," quipped Nuala as she made way for Judith. Gwendoline grinned happily as she took Judith's money for Pink Carnation.

Fidelma hurried over to the table. "One for me and one for Aileen," she said. "Belladonna, please."

"It's a rank outsider. Hasn't a chance," Monica felt impelled to warn her, but Fidelma only took her ticket and went quickly back to get a good place in front of the television.

The last girl had hardly received her ticket from Gwendoline when it was time for the race to begin. There was a mad scramble for seats and a lot of girls ended up sitting on the floor.

A hushed silence fell until the gate was lifted, and the horses raced out and along the course. As at least three or even four girls had betted on each horse and each of them felt that their particular horse needed constant vocal encouragement to perform well, the din in the common room was terrific.

Pink Carnation led most of the way with Pride of

Blackrock, Bootpolish and Mr Pickles keeping very close behind him. This kept up until the last straight and then Bootpolish and Mr Pickles drew well ahead. Everyone was resigned to the fact that one or other of them would win, but suddenly Belladonna, the outsider, overtook the leaders and got ahead. Bootpolish couldn't keep up the pace but Mr Pickles made a gallant effort, and the two horses thundered neck-and-neck towards the winning post. It was hard to know whose horse had won, though the majority of the girls thought it must have been Belladonna.

A minute later it was confirmed. Just as the commentator announced, "Winner all right," Aileen rushed into the room.

"What's going on here?" she cried. "Sr Gobnait is on her way up to find out what all the noise is about."

Judith rushed forward and switched off the television, but not before the nearest girls could see a smart-looking woman who looked vaguely familiar standing beside Belladonna. "The victor being congratulated by Countess . . . " were the last words they heard. Then everyone made an effort at tidying the room and tried to look as if they had been sitting quietly all this time.

Gwendoline got so excited that she tore the racing page out of her science copy and stuffed it into her pocket. Then she threw the copy into one of the presses which lined the wall.

Someone shouted, "Nuala sing something, quickly!"

Nuala was a bit taken aback by this but she obediently opened her mouth and sang the first thing that came into her head.

"Morning has broken . . . " being sung beautifully by Nuala to an attentive audience was the astonishing sight which met Sr Gobnait's eyes when she opened the common room door.

"That was lovely, Nuala," she said, "quite lovely," when the clapping had died down. "But I think a quick jog around the hockey pitch would do you all good. It's stopped raining and you've just time before tea."

She stood at the common room door until the last girl had left it, looking as if something was puzzling her a lot.

As Aileen and Fidelma jogged around the pitch, they rejoiced at the good news which had just been confirmed by Gwendoline. She had pulled out the now rather grubby piece of paper on the way out and revealed that Aileen and Fidelma were the only winners.

"In fact," she informed them, "you scooped the lot, about £16 anyway."

"This is my lucky month," gloated Aileen. "Last week I won two pounds over Nuala's cake and now another eight pounds."

"The funny thing is that we're the only winners," said Fidelma. "Why did no one else bet on Belladonna?"

"It never won a race before," explained Josie. "Monica told us all about each horse's form beforehand."

"I was in the parlour then, lucky me" sighed Aileen. "It was the name which appealed to me."

Tea was nearly over before Nuala remembered that Aileen had had visitors that afternoon.

"How's your mother, Aileen?" she asked as she passed milk to her.

"Fine," replied Aileen pouring the milk in her tea. "That reminds me, I never told you about David ringing me, Mum coming put it out of my mind."

"Your cousin David?" asked Josie.

"Yes, he and his friend Paul found out from Mr Greene the list of places we will be going to on the Boynepeace outings. So to liven up our lives they have buried treasure in one of the sites. He is sending us a map with clues on it. I hope the treasure isn't something awful, you know what boys are like."

"Brilliant. It'll save us the bother of doing something about it ourselves," Josie commented cheerfully.

"Won't the boys be there too? I don't fancy looking for clues with them around," protested Nuala.

"Apparently not. It was the first thing I asked too. He says Miss Crilly told Mr Greene that she thought it would be better if we didn't meet again, so they are going the day before us each week, that's what made them think of the treasure idea."

"You mean she doesn't want to meet Mr Greene herself," Eithne pointed out cynically. "I wonder what he did to make her so angry with him."

After tea a distraught Gwendoline met Aileen

and Fidelma on the stairs. "I've just been up in the common room," she sobbed, "and the race money has disappeared. I had it in a little green suede bag, and they've both gone."

"Sr Gobnait must have seen them lying around and taken them," suggested Monica soothingly. "Go down and ask her now. You don't have to tell her what the money was for."

A harassed-looking Gwendoline left then, only to return about ten minutes later with the news that Sr Gobnait had not only denied all knowledge of the money, but had asked her some searching questions about its presence in the common room.

"I feel drained, utterly drained," she confided to Monica, her closest friend later that night. "Only we've a break this weekend, I don't think I'd last out."

"I know how you feel," agreed Monica. "Talking about the weekend, Ciara told me that Lisa Shevlin and Sharon Kennedy are spending the weekend in Dublin with Lisa's sister Maria, who is a med. student in UCD. Anyway Maria and her boyfriend are taking Lisa and Sharon to a nightclub on Friday night. Promise not to tell anyone as they don't want it to get back to Sr Gobnait."

"They're going to a nightclub in Dublin and they're only in fifth year?" remarked Gwendoline bitterly. "When I think of the lecture Sr Gobnait gave me on the wickedness of leaving money lying around and putting temptation in people's way. It just makes me sick."

10

Questions and Quotes

"The Hot Potato is the 'in' nightclub at the moment," Maria had told Lisa and Sharon earlier in the evening. Now following her down the entry stairs and into the club, they could certainly believe it. The low-ceilinged room they now entered was noisy and black with people.

Maria and Neil, her boyfriend, pushed and shoved their way through the room, past the crowded bar and over to an alcove where they managed to grab a table for the four of them. Lisa and Sharon, following close behind them, wished that the rest of fifth year could see them now.

As Sharon squeezed herself past a table to get to her seat, she couldn't help noticing the people who were sitting there. A slim blonde girl whose companion, well-dressed and black-haired, was obviously foreign. Her eyes widened at the size of the champagne bottle the waiter was opening for them.

The room was so noisy that most people were shouting so as to be heard by the person next to them. She dropped into the seat next to Lisa, only to hear the blonde girl laughingly shout, "You're over in Ireland looking for a girl and you say that she's your cousin? A likely story, I don't believe a word of it." She couldn't hear the man's reply.

After a while Neil and Maria got up to dance on the tiny dance floor. Sharon watched them and the coloured lights playing over the dancers. Though she wouldn't have admitted it even to herself, the heavy smoke-laden atmosphere, throbbing with over-loud music and noisy voices was giving her a blinding headache. She sipped her orange juice feeling rather flat.

Just then Lisa shouted in her ear, "Isn't this brilliant!" and she replied, "Fabulous."

Maria came back with a few friends who squashed in between the girls. Sharon moved up to make room for them and found herself beside the blonde girl who was drinking champagne.

"Where did you say your cousin's school was?" the blonde was shouting to the man, who shouted back, "I don't know where it is, on a river somewhere, Saint something or other . . . yes . . . Brigid's, that's it."

The blonde burst out laughing. "It could be anywhere, Brigid is a very common Irish name."

The man caught sight of Sharon's startled face. "Forget it," he ordered harshly. "I've got someone working on it anyway."

Sharon, who had jumped when she heard the name of the school, looked covertly at him, observing his brown skin and rather harsh features. What country would he be from . . . the Persian

Gulf, Iran or Iraq? She wondered could his cousin be at their St Brigid's but came to the conclusion that as nobody at the school came from those countries it was unlikely.

Lisa nudged her and she turned back to her friends. A short time later she was asked to dance by Neil and when she got back to her place again, she noticed the pair at the next table had gone.

As the following Monday was a bank holiday the boarders hadn't to be back until eight PM. Some time after seven on that evening, Aileen, Natalie, Judith and the twins were going downstairs, talking and laughing as Lisa and Sharon were going up to their own dormitory. They had just arrived back from their exciting weekend in Dublin.

Normally Lisa and Sharon wouldn't have paid any attention to a group of third years. On this occasion however as the two groups passed each other on the stairs Natalie asked Aileen when would she show them the contents of her letter from Newgrange College. It was fairly quiet on the stairs for once and Natalie's voice with its strong foreign intonation struck Sharon as unusual. She looked at the new girl, taking in her strikingly different appearance.

As they turned into the dormitory corridor, they met Nuala who was hurrying down to join her friends.

"Hey Nuala," Sharon called roughly, "is that dark-haired girl in your year an Arab from the Gulf or something like that?"

"I don't know what you're talking about," replied Nuala in a cold but dignified voice. Sharon Kennedy was no favourite of hers.

"You know who I mean. She has very long black hair and a brown face with great big eyes," Sharon said impatiently.

"If you mean Natalie Frossart, she's from Scotland as far as I know. Anyway, what's it to you?"

"Nothing, except that I heard in Dublin that her cousin was looking for her. He wasn't sure where St Brigid's was. That's all," said Sharon shortly, nettled by the unfriendly look on Nuala's face. Then she swept off after Lisa who, getting bored, had gone ahead.

"Third years, a mob of intellectual inferiors," she was muttering to Lisa when the dormitory door opened. A crowd of fifth years came out and fell upon them with cries of "Did you get to a night club?" and "What was the night club like?"

Nuala, looking thoughtful and rather grim, ran down the stairs to the common room. As she neared it Aileen looked out the door and called, "Come on, Nuala, we are all here now. I've got David's letter and we all want to hear what's in it."

Nuala, putting the thoughts which Sharon's question had raised in her mind to one side for the present, called back cheerfully, "Keep your hair on, Aileen, I'm coming as quick as I can!"

Aileen took a piece of folded paper out of an envelope and spread it out on the common room table. Josie peered over her shoulders and asked, "Where's the map? All I can see is a list of names."

"They list the places we're going to," began Aileen, when Josie interrupted again.

"Where's Pearlach Wood? I've never heard of it," she asked.

"That's where we're going to on Wednesday."

"Really, Josie!" expostulated Aileen. "Go away and let me read my own letter. Pearlach Wood is situated near Newgrange College. The boys will be going there tomorrow and they'll leave a clue for us there. To help us find this clue they enclosed a little rhyme for us – here it is:

'Ancient boiler now disused, Which stone is it? Yours to choose.'"

She looked around at the bewildered faces of her friends.

"It's no use looking at me," said Monica. "I can't even do the simplest crossword."

"I think we'd better wait until we get to Pearlach Wood," said Nuala. "Read out the rest of the letter."

"'Carraigphooca, Monasterboice and Calfe's Pool'," Aileen read out obediently. "If we find the clues in each of the four places, we can put them together. Read correctly and we will know where the treasure is hidden. 'One warning – the clues are all mixed up. They're not in the order of each place'."

She looked around at them. "What do you think, should we bother?"

"Of course, we can't let the boys beat us," Josie immediately answered. "We'll just have to find the grotty treasure."

"But where are these places?" asked a bewildered Natalie.

"Carraigphooca is a big meadow-like place, way beyond the playing fields," replied Nuala.

"You've been to Calfe's Pool," chimed in Fidelma, "and Monasterboice is an ancient monastery site with a round tower, not far from here."

"We are all agreed to look for the treasure then?" asked Aileen.

"Yes," replied Judith. "Especially since Nuala discovered from Miss Ryan that we would need a special licence to get a metal detector. Isn't that right, Nuala?"

"Yes, indeed. Miss Ryan says that the law has been tightened up since some people using a detector found a chalice down south somewhere."

"Did you tell her what we wanted it for?" asked Josie.

Nuala was shocked. "Certainly not. I merely showed her my essay and asked her advice. She was only to happy to oblige."

"Wednesday is going to be very full this week," said Eithne. "When we get back from Pearlach wood we have a tennis lesson with the stunning Steve."

Natalie's face brightened up at this. She loved tennis lessons while Boynepeace bored her to tears.

The door opened and Rachel Quinn, another of their year, came in and announced in a loud voice, "Sr Gobnait says that if anyone would like refreshments they are being served in the refectory."

"Iced coffee maybe or chilled *Jungle* with

84

strawberries and cream would be nice. What about you, Judith?" asked Nuala.

"Perhaps we'd better go down to make sure that she's chilling the drinks properly," suggested Judith. "Anyone coming?"

Rachel laughed. "There's milk, orange juice and tea with plain biscuits."

"I don't believe you!" cried Aileen. "Natalie is very fond of iced lemon tea. I'd better run down and tell Sr Gobnait."

She left the common room ahead of the others and was back in a few minutes panting. "Listen everyone, there a notice up about the school tour. This year it's Rome! What do you think of that?"

They all hurried down to see the notice for themselves.

11

Natalie Tells All

Nuala looked with satisfaction at the diagram of the human heart which she had drawn on her answer paper. Swiftly she filled in the names of each of its various parts. Having checked her paper carefully she wrote "vena cava" in its place with a flourish.

"That's done, thank goodness," she murmured to herself as she put her pen down and looked around the silent classroom. Everyone else seemed to be still engrossed in finishing the biology test.

Miss Crilly consulted her watch and announced gravely, "Only five minutes left." Then she called Nuala up to her desk.

"I see you're finished, Nuala. Would you take this note down to Miss Ryan in the staffroom, please," she requested pleasantly.

Nuala handed over her test papers and set off with alacrity to deliver the teacher's note. It was when she was returning back upstairs again, her mission accomplished, that she decided to stop and look out of the huge oriel window on the second landing. This gave an excellent view of a small formal garden which lay at the back of the castle.

As she admired the smooth clipped hedges and bright flower-beds she noticed a man walking slowly through it. He seemed familiar, but she couldn't quite place where she had seen him before. She was still trying to remember when she reached the classroom again. Biology class was over and Miss Crilly had already left.

Sr Imelda's arrival shortly afterwards drove the whole incident from her mind, especially as the nun had plenty of criticisms of the previous week's work. English class was further enlivened by Josie who tripped over something as she returned to her place, having collected the copy books for Sr Imelda. She fell quite heavily on her right arm necessitating a visit to the infirmary. She only arrived back in time for the end of class, but in her usual good spirits with the afflicted limb nestling comfortably in a sling.

"Would you like me to cut up your meat for you, Josie?" asked Judith kindly as they walked into the refectory for dinner.

"No thanks," replied Josie cheerfully. "I can manage quite well. I'm only wearing this silly sling because Sr Joseph insisted on it."

"It looks most impressive, it's a pity your face isn't all white and haggard to match it," Nuala commented as they sat down to eat.

"You could put on some white powder," suggested Aileen. "But if you're not up to eating your dessert, I'll eat it for you. I heard a rumour that it was going to be Black Forest Gateau today."

Josie laughed. "No fear of that, I'm not sick, just a bit sore. The best thing is that Sr Joseph told me not to go to art class this afternoon. She suggested that I should just sit quietly in the garden instead."

Judith, who loved art, looked sympathetically at her and advised, "Learn your Shakespeare, Sr Imelda gave us reams to do tonight."

"That reminds me, I haven't a singing lesson today, Mr Lynch is away to Rome for two weeks," Nuala mentioned. "I wonder could I join Josie in the garden?"

"The thing to do," advised Judith, "is to ask Sr Gobnait should you go out in the garden to keep an eye on Josie in case she gets weak or anything like that. Look worried as you ask her, then she'll think you ought to go with her."

"That's a brilliant idea. Nuala, will you do it?" asked Josie hopefully.

"Why not? I've nothing to lose," argued Nuala. "But somehow I don't think Gobnait will be taken in that easily."

However, Sr Gobnait when approached thought it was a good idea too. She seemed preoccupied, and uncharacteristically gave permission without asking any awkward questions of Nuala.

So, while the others went off to the art room for the rest of the afternoon, Josie and Nuala armed with *Henry IV*, Part One went jubilantly into the garden and took possession of one of the many wooden seats there.

For the first thirty minutes or so they studied

diligently. Then Josie yawned and complained, "The sun's very hot here isn't it?"

"Is your arm hurting you a lot?" asked Nuala.

"No, my arm's just fine," replied Josie, "but I'm very thirsty. What I'd really love is an ice cream. A whipped cone, all soft and creamy. I can't stop thinking about it."

"I'd love one myself. Don't tempt me, Josie. You know we'd have to go to the village for one of those and it's out of bounds."

"I know that but I'd just love one all the same," was her reply.

They took up *Henry IV* again. About ten minutes later Josie saw Nuala look at her watch, then at her and then at her watch again.

"The sun is very hot here. Let's move over to that bench over there," suggested Nuala and she pointed to a seat quite a distance away.

Josie was surprised. "The sun isn't that hot," she demurred.

"Well," pronounced Nuala, "if you want to cut a quick dash down to the village for that ice cream cone, we'll have to move first to another seat that isn't overlooked by the whole school."

Josie gave a pleased laugh. "It's an awful risk but it's worth it. Let's move." She got up and picked up her books.

"Lean on me," ordered Nuala, "and for goodness sake, try and look delicate. I'll lead you over to that seat in case any busybody is looking."

Nuala insisted on waiting five minutes before they moved to another seat, even further from the vicinity of prying eyes.

Eventually Nuala felt it was safe for them to slip down to the village. They set off at a brisk pace and soon reached the ice cream shop. As they were waiting for someone to serve them Nuala suddenly remembered who the man she had seen in the garden was.

"Professor Jenkins, that's who it was!" she told a mystified Josie.

"Professor Jenkins . . . who is Professor Jenkins?" asked Josie in a puzzled voice.

"If you are looking for Professor Jenkins," said the shopkeeper, suddenly materialising beside them, "he's out in the street there, look," and she pointed to the large shop window behind them. Nuala swung around but Josie, deciding that she couldn't wait any longer for their ice cream, ordered two large cones.

"What a coincidence . . . " Nuala started to say, but the words died on her lips as she looked out the window and saw the man in question deep in conversation with the very woman she had run away from that day in the museum, still wearing the floppy hat and bright pink coat.

"The woman in pink!" she gasped as she shrank back from the window.

"Is there another way out of here?" she whispered to Josie who stared in amazement at her white face.

"What's the matter, Nuala?" she asked in a concerned voice. "What did you see out there?"

Just then a group of people came noisily into the

shop, laughing and talking and blocking out their views of the street. When Nuala peeped out again she saw to her relief that Professor Jenkins and the women were now walking into the *Boyne Arms*, which was situated a little further down the street on the opposite side to the shop.

At this stage Josie, clutching two melting icecreams in her good hand, was urging her to leave. Nuala snatched one of the cones from her.

"Come on, Josie, let's go quickly while there's time!" she cried. Then she hurried out of the shop door closely followed by her sorely-tried friend. As they trotted back to school Nuala, between hasty licks of icecream, told Josie all about Professor Jenkins and also about her chilling encounter with the pink-coated women in the museum.

"Golly, Nuala, do you think she's traced you here for a purpose?" asked Josie excitedly. She finished off the last bit of cone and then scrubbed her hands with a tissue.

"I don't know. What on earth could she want me for? I remember she mentioned something that day in the museum. It's hopeless, I can't recall what it was," replied Nuala plainly annoyed with herself.

"Eithne was with you in the museum. Maybe she will help to remember it. I suppose you'll tell the others about the woman with the professor?"

"Definitely, there must be some significance in it," said Nuala, who had stopped to wipe her face and hands. "Ice cream is delicious, but drippy, I feel sticky all over."

"Me too," said Josie.

By this time they had reached the playing fields. Skirting these and keeping close to the dense row of shrubs which lined the drive they arrived safely back in the garden. They had hardly seated themselves again, when the bell went for the end of afternoon school. It wasn't long before they were joined by Aileen, Judith, Eithne and Fidelma Murray.

"What were you two doing dodging from seat to seat?" asked Aileen as she flopped down on the warm grass beside the white bench.

"Sr Patrick looked out the art room window and was riveted by the sight of your bench-hopping. She called me over and asked me if that was the latest way to cure sore arms."

"It was the sun," explained Nuala, avoiding Josie's amused eyes. "The sun was too hot for poor Josie, so we moved around for a cooler position."

"A likely story," Aileen retorted. "I suppose you were really trying to slip quietly away to the village for something."

This time Nuala joined in the laughter. "How did you guess Josie was dying for an icecream?" she asked.

"I know your ways," grinned Aileen. "Though I must admit it was only a guess. Did you see anything exciting there?"

"Well as it happens she did," said Josie. "Go on, Nuala, tell them what you saw."

Nuala's story caused quite a sensation. "I wish I could remember the name she asked me about,"

Nuala fretted out loud when everyone had finished expressing their opinions on the subject.

"Could it have been Natalia El Khadi?" asked a fresh voice from behind them, causing everyone to jump and Judith to fall off the back of the bench where she had been precariously perched.

"Oh Natalie!" cried Josie. "Why did you creep up like that behind us? It gave us all a terrible fright."

"I didn't creep up, it was just that you didn't hear me coming across the grass," the newcomer explained indignantly.

"Say that name again!" ordered Nuala. "It rings a bell."

"Natalia El Khadi."

"That's it!" cried Nuala. "Do you know this person by any chance?"

Natalie smiled wryly. "I suppose you could say I do . . . it's me . . . I mean I'm her . . . " she said.

"You're her!" exclaimed Nuala in astonishment. "You mean that awful woman is looking for *you*? Why?"

Natalie hesitated, looking a bit mulish and uncooperative. Before she could say anything, Judith, none the worse from her fall on the grass, looked up from picking bits of grass off her uniform and said, "I think you should tell us what's going on, we might be able to help, you know."

Though they were all bursting with curiosity, the others held their peace, as various expressions crossed Natalie's face. Finally Josie moved over on the seat and said coaxingly, "Come on, Natalie, sit down here between Nuala and myself and tell us your story. You've no idea how much experience we have in getting the better of things. When we've more time I'll tell you all about the adventures of J O'Leary and the countess."

Natalie seemed to come to some decision. Seating herself between the two friends she announced, "I will tell you why I am here and why that woman is looking for me." She said nothing for a minute, just looked across at the groups of girls sitting on the grass, or walking up and down enjoying the sun and their free time.

"It's like another world here," she murmured. Then she shook herself and began her tale. "My cousins call me Natalia El Khadi, but I have always been Natalie Frossart. I suppose you've guessed that I'm not from Scotland really. My father, who was a doctor and died when I was a baby, was also a son of Prince Sadrudden Ben. You might have heard of him."

Judith looked at her. "I certainly have," she cried. "During the Easter holidays the English papers were full of news about him and his nephews. Gosh, Natalie, you're not the missing girl who they want to marry off to some big shot, are you?"

Natalie laughed, pleased at the awed look on the faces of the girls around her.

"It's like a film, isn't it? It wouldn't have happened only my grandfather got sick and my cousins thought they would start taking over. You see, I inherited everything from Father. Anyway, my mother was warned that they might kidnap me. She had been at school with Sr Gobnait years ago. When she rang her up, Gobnait advised her to send me here. They didn't think anyone would ever look for me at St Brigid's. I'm really amazed that they even found out about this place at all."

"Maybe all they know is that it's a school called St Brigid's somewhere in Ireland," suggested Josie, "so they're probably going through all the schools."

"No" objected Judith. "Only boarding schools and there's not many left any more."

"If you keep near the school, they won't see you," Aileen said thoughtfully. "I suppose . . . "

"No," cried Nuala, jumping up. "I promised my mother not to get involved again. What we are going to do, Natalie, is go straight to dear Sr Gobberlets and tell her about the Woman in Pink in the museum who has now turned up in the village. Come on, she'll know what to do."

Though the others thought it was a dull and spineless way of doing things, they all agreed in the end that Nuala was right.

"Don't breathe a word to anyone until we come back," warned Nuala. "It might be dangerous for Natalie."

The two girls set out to look for Sr Gobnait. They tried the office first, where she was usually to be found at this hour, but when they got there Mary Jones, the head girl, was sitting there explaining to everyone that Sr Gobnait wasn't available.

"Why not?" asked Nuala in a disappointed voice.

"She's gone to attend a special teachers' conference. They are meeting the Minister for Education tomorrow, so she won't be back for a few days," explained Mary, "but if your problem is urgent I am sure Sr Imelda will do her best to help you solve it."

"No thanks," was Nuala's immediate reply, echoed by Natalie. "It will wait until Sr Gobnait returns."

The two girls left the office and hastened back to the garden to break the news to the others.

"We'll have to watch Natalie all the time," suggested Josie. "It's just as well she's in Ita's dorm, isn't it?" she added when Nuala had finished telling the bad news about the nun's absence from the school.

"That's a good idea," agreed Aileen. "But we'll have to watch out for any strangers hanging around too."

"You're right, Aileen," said Nuala. "I think we should tell Monica and Gwendoline too, because they're in the dorm as well, but we'll really have to swear not to talk about it even between ourselves. If it got around the school, you know the whole country would know in no time at all."

"You are all very kind," an obviously embarrassed Natalie said stiffly, "but of course there may be no need to worry. This woman in pink is probably a private detective hired by my cousins and if I keep near the school, she won't see me."

"She wouldn't want to," Eithne pointed out

crisply. "You stick out a mile, Natalie. Look around you, everyone looks much the same, fuzzy curly hair, pale faces, lumpy uniformed figures, socks around ankles, but you have enormous eyes in a tanned face and your hair – just look at the length of it – and its colour, black and glossy."

Judith laughed at the horrified look on Natalie's face. "After that description, aren't you glad you're different from us?" she said. "But she's right about your hair, it does stick out."

"There's the tea bell," announced Fidelma. "Come on, you lumpy-figured fuzzy-wuzzies, it's time to go in."

"Remember, no talking!" warned Nuala. "I'll tell Monica and Gwendoline after tea. I hope we can trust them to keep their mouths shut, especially Monica."

12

Steve's Mishap

The following morning Miss Ryan took the class to Pearlach Wood. As it was situated about five miles away from the school, they travelled by coach.

At first Natalie's self-appointed custodians kept a sharp look-out for any suspicious-looking strangers on the road, but as they didn't pass even one person on the way there, they soon relaxed and forgot about the danger.

Pearlach Wood did not impress the girls.

"It's not much of a place, is it?" pronounced Aileen, looking at the tall pines which soared above them. "Dark, gloomy and kind of dead."

"I couldn't agree more," said Nuala who was walking with Aileen on one side of her, and Judith on the other.

"The only living thing here appears to be the ivy climbing up the tree-trunks. Even our footsteps are muted."

"I wonder what Miss Ryan is going to show us?" said Judith.

It soon became apparent that the wood was coming to an end. Minutes later they streamed thankfully out of it, and into the sunshine again. A large meadow-like place lay in front of them, leading down to a narrow river.

Miss Ryan was waiting for them there.

As soon as the last girls joined, the group gathered around her and she announced, "I know you've all been wondering why I brought you here today. It was to show this recently excavated *Fulachta Fiadh*," and she pointed to a horseshoe-shaped mound. In front of this there was a deep pit in the earth, and the girls could see that it was lined with old planks of wood. To one side of this there were some piles of blackened stones.

"This is what our ancestors cooked their meat in," the teacher informed them. "They filled up the trough with water from the river. Then they heated the stones in the fire, until they were red-hot. These they carefully rolled into the water-filled trough. This had the effect of boiling the water. Then meat, wrapped in unthreshed oats, would be placed in the boiling water until it was cooked."

"Did it really cook the meat?" asked Ciara in a sceptical voice. "I can't believe that, it doesn't seem possible."

"Certainly it did. They have done experiments and proved it. There are hundreds of these all over the country. Some are quite small, but others are big enough for a whole village to use for a celebration meal. Before I let you wander around for a better look, I must warn you to be careful and not to damage anything."

They all promised to be careful. Then they

formed more or less into a double line and walked slowly around looking at the site. Some of the girls found it interesting but quite a few couldn't see what all the fuss was about. Others commented loudly on how relieved they were that more modern ways of cooking meat had been developed.

Miss Ryan was explaining to Josie, Aileen and a few of the more interested girls about how people had flung stones to one side after they had finished using them. After many years these stones had formed the horseshoe-shaped mound around the pit. Judith, standing at the back of this group, noticed a pile of stone pieces which had obviously only recently been excavated. As she looked idly at them she was struck by an oddly-shaped stone amongst the cracked and shattered remains there. It was also coloured a particularly virulent shade of green.

Everyone appeared to be looking at Miss Ryan, so Judith bent down and picked up the strange object. It was as light as paper, but to her dismay when she prodded it slightly, it just fell to pieces in her hand. As she was desperately wondering what terrible penalty she would incur by destroying such an ancient and valuable piece of heritage, she noticed the paper among the bits.

She pulled the paper out furtively and was surprised to see in crabbed writing 'In ye year of ye lord MXXLIII', written by an unmistakable twentieth-century Biro. This brought back to her mind the boys' treasure puzzle which they had all forgotten about in the excitement of hearing Natalie's story.

Aileen slithered over beside her and whispered dramatically, "I've cracked it, this is the ancient boiler mentioned in the clue, but which of the millions of stones here is the right one?"

Judith silently handed her the piece of paper which she had found.

Aileen gave a startled yip – "Brilliant, how did you find it?" – before she carefully placed it in a purse which she then returned to her pocket.

"Just luck," replied Judith. "I'll tell you the whole story later. I think we're going now."

There was great jubilation among the friends on the way home.

"I wonder what it means. MXXLIII is Roman numerals, a date would you think?" Nuala asked Aileen sitting beside her in the coach.

"I don't know Roman numerals, we'll have to look it up," Aileen replied taking the precious piece of paper out of her purse. She unfolded it carefully and read out:

"'Whe ref Ivet Reesg Ro Wog Eth.'

What's that all about?" she exclaimed.

Nuala read the strange words. "I haven't an idea. Put it away, Aileen, we'll have to have a meeting and discuss it later."

"All right," agreed Aileen amiably. "I suppose it's a bit too public here anyway."

However, when they arrived back at the castle they hadn't time to discuss anything as Sharon Kennedy was waiting impatiently for them at the locker room door.

"You're late," she snapped at them. "Hurry up

and get changed and out on the courts quickly. Steve sent me to tell you he's waiting." With that she left the locker room.

There was a lot of grumbling and complaining about Sharon Kennedy and her bossy ways, as everyone changed as quickly as possible.

"There's a name for Sharon K, but I won't sully your ears with it," pronounced Josie thoughtfully as she tied back her abundant locks.

"Thank goodness for that," murmured Nuala. "It's bad enough finding your watch is ten minutes slow, when you bought a battery only a few weeks ago."

"That's funny. Mine is slow too," cried Judith. A quick survey of the room revealed that everyone's watch was apparently slow too. Steve must have made a mistake.

"It's that Sharon," fumed Deirdre as they hurried out to the tennis courts. "I bet she made the whole thing up."

"I wouldn't be surprised," agreed Monica.

It was Steve's usual practice to finish each tennis lesson with a doubles match, comprising three of the girls and himself. This particular week it was the turn of Monica, Gwendoline and Natalie to play the match with him. Because Natalie was such a strong player, Steve asked the highly flattered Monica to be his partner.

It turned out to be a good match, going on longer than expected. By this time the whole class were hanging around the court, taking sides and cheering at appropriate times.

Just as the game finished Sharon Kennedy bustled

out all business to tell Steve that he was wanted on the phone. He had started to do his usual leap over the net to shake hands with his opponents, when he was distracted by the bossy fifth year, causing him to catch his foot in the net and fall heavily to the ground. A horrified silence fell on the onlookers, especially when they saw a large piece of Steve's thick hair detach itself from his head, and fly across the court coming to land at the feet of the dumbstruck Sharon. She numbly picked up the fair toupee and walked over like an automaton to the unfortunate coach, who was sitting up rubbing an ankle and looking dazed. She handed it to him, then put her hands up to her face and screamed and rushed back to the castle again, quite forgetting to give him the message from Sr Imelda that he was wanted on the telephone.

Natalie ran over to Steve. "Are you badly hurt?" she cried. "Will I get a doctor?"

The tennis coach got gingerly to his feet and walked around. "No, I'm just fine." He had jammed his hair back on quickly, when Sharon had given it to him, so that the girls wouldn't notice any difference, except that in his agitation he had put it on the wrong way around. It made quite a few girls feel light-headed and giggly. It was obvious that it wouldn't take much to start them laughing loudly.

Fortunately Sr Imelda came out looking very worried after the hysterical tale Sharon had brought in to her. She bore the coach away into the castle and the dangerous moment passed.

Steve's fall was the talk of the refectory. The room buzzed with comment, not all of it complimentary.

Natalie summed up the general feeling of the school when she spoke about it at her table. "Steve's hair must have fallen out after a severe illness. He needs to wear a toupee only until his own hair grows back again." As she was a doctor's daughter, everyone agreed she must be right.

Later that evening Steve went into the *Boyne Arms*. He ordered a drink and then sat down in one of the high-backed seats in the far corner of the almost empty pub.

He wasn't long there when he was disturbed by a voice saying warmly, "Why it must be Steve Honeycombe. My dear fellow, I saw you playing at Wimbledon a few years ago in that great match where you beat Jimmy Cash."

Steve looked with surprise at the man in front of him.

"My name is Jenkins, PR," said the newcomer. "Call me Percy. May I join you?"

"Hi," Steve replied and waved a hand at the seat opposite him. "Do by all means."

Some drinks later Steve told Percy about his mishap at St Brigid's earlier that day. Both men laughed genially about it.

"That reminds me, Steve, have you ever come across a girl in that school called Natalie Frossart?" Percy asked casually.

Steve looked surprised. "Why?" he asked.

"I just wondered. Her mother and father were great friends of mine," said PR Jenkins blandly.

13

Carraigphooca

"Where's Judith?" asked Nuala climbing nimbly on to her favourite branch in the big beech tree.

"Sr Patrick wanted her for something. She'll be out soon, I expect," answered Aileen absently. She was studying David's letter yet again in the hope that it might cast some light on the cryptic message which they had picked up the previous week in the *Fulachta Fiadh*. Apart from working out the date of the year was 1253, they had failed to get any meaning from it. Nuala and Judith had even searched diligently in the library to see if anything relevant had happened in the history of the area about the year 1253, but to no avail.

"You're an optimist, Aileen," pronounced Eithne "if you think you'll find any help in that old letter."

"You never know," replied Aileen. "It looks as if we'll have to get the other three clues before we can work the thing out. This letter says that they are all jumbled up."

"Maybe you're right," agreed Eithne. "What do you think, Nuala?"

Nuala, watching the soft greenish light cast by the sun filtering in through the fresh young beech leaves all around them, answered thoughtfully, "I think it's like living in an undersea cave myself, don't you . . . "

Eithne, Fidelma, Aileen and even Natalie laughed at her reply, but Josie dismissed this flight of fancy brusquely.

"Don't be a twit, Nuala. Anyway I've just remembered that it's a week since the woman in pink was last sighted. Do you think that she has gone somewhere else and that Natalie is safe going out on the Boynepeace outings?"

"I don't care what the woman in pink does, now that Sr Gobnait has returned to St B's," observed Nuala cheerfully.

"It's a good thing Carraigphooca is in our own grounds all the same," remarked Aileen.

"What's Carraigphooca?" asked Natalie.

"The rock of the fairies, I suppose," explained Nuala. "According to Miss Crilly, it's a perfect example of a natural meadow untouched by pollution. That means tomorrow she'll show us a big field full of long grass, with cornflowers, red poppies and stinging nettles in it. She'll go on about the fact that it's never had artificial fertilisers on it too. She's mad about that sort of place, isn't she, Aileen?"

"Yes, but I'm getting used to this green stuff, especially as it's miles better than class," grinned Aileen. "And don't forget we have to get that second clue too."

"I know. We've just got to beat the boys," observed Josie firmly, "but what worries me is their treasure. It could easily be a dead rat or even a few smelly old football socks, Dennis the Menace stuff."

Natalie wrinkled up her nose and cried, "Ugh, disgusting!" A sentiment which all the other girls agreed heartily with except Aileen, who only laughed at them.

"We'll just have to wait and see," she chuckled.

"Well, if the treasure is either of those things," promised Eithne fiercely, "I'll personally wreak my vengeance on the pair of them."

"Hear, hear!" cried Fidelma. "I'm with you there."

Judith's head appeared among the beech foliage. "Hi gang!" she called gaily. Aileen moved over and made space for her.

Judith swung up on the branch and seated herself gratefully beside Josie, who asked, "What did Sr Patrick want you for?"

"She has a plan to clear out the greenroom presses, you know, the place just behind the stage, and sort out all the costumes and props there. It hasn't been done for years apparently. I offered to help and she jumped at it."

"I'll lend a hand too," said Nuala. "It might be a bit of crack."

"Me too," agreed Aileen.

Eithne looked worried. "If it's on the half day this week I can't join in," she said. "I promised Gráinne I'd go to the *Slógadh* finals in Dundalk with her and Fidelma. Gráinne's sister is in the fifth year piece. Aren't you coming too, Josie?"

"Oh blow, I'd forgotten all about it. I'll have to go, I promised Gráinne too. I would have liked to have rooted around the greenroom presses."

"Pity about that," commented Judith. "I expect Sr Patrick will scoop in a few more to help, especially as Sr Gobnait is behind it too."

"There's a rumour going around that the major wants all the presses in common rooms to be cleaned out as well," warned Josie.

"You're not serious! I can't see why she doesn't wait until the end of term," grumbled Fidelma crossly.

Natalie, realising that she might be sent to the *Slógadh* finals if she didn't watch out, decided on the lesser of two evils. "I'll help too, Judith," she said graciously, "but I have to say we never cleaned presses or did dirty work like that in my last school. They had cleaners for that sort of thing."

Nobody made any comment but the other girls thought what Nuala put into words later, as they were going into Study. "That Scottish school is getting to be the most perfect school in the world."

The following morning most of Miss Crilly's peroration on the beauty of the Carraigphooca meadow and the importance of banning all garden and field-spraying insecticides fell on deaf ears. Most of the girls were fully occupied in looking around and discreetly searching for the next clue in the treasure stakes.

Ironically, it was the teacher who found it for

them in the end. She had just finished speaking and was leading the class away from the meadow proper. Suddenly she gave an exclamation of displeasure and darted forward, plucking something out of the ground surrounding the large group of rocks which gave the place its name. A tiny waterfall splashing down through the rocks had created an area of boggy ground, now pretty with masses of primroses and marsh marigolds.

"Plastic! How did it get here?" fumed the teacher, holding up the abhorred object.

Aileen who was standing near her got a clear view of this piece of plastic. Immediately she guessed who the culprits were.

To everyone's amazement she ran over and snatched the piece of plastic from the teacher's upraised hand shouting as she did so: "Disgusting vandals! Give it to me – I'll get rid of it for you."

She ran back to Nuala thrusting something into her hand and making faces at her. Then she turned back to the teacher and said, "It's only a plastic bag, Miss Crilly. It's very clean. Leave it to me; I'll recycle it."

Miss Crilly who had been too surprised to even reprimand Aileen, now spoke in a pleased voice.

"I am delighted to see what an improvement Boynepeace has made in you, Aileen. Recycling the plastic bag is an excellent idea. I hope the rest of you learn from this."

Aileen had the grace to blush at this quite unmerited praise, especially as the others were looking at her with amazement on their faces.

Nuala murmured wickedly, "It's quite true, she is the sort whose heart dies a little whenever she sees plastic bags thrown at the side of the road. Pollution actually hurts her."

"More of that and I'll pollute your leg with a kick," hissed Aileen, quite forgetting her momentary embarrassment.

Later on as they straggled back to the castle, Nuala and Aileen managed a quick look at the paper which Aileen had pulled out of the plastic bag and had thrust at Nuala. All they could see of it was, "Ye treasure of ye Boyne. MDCXIII" but it was sufficient.

Aileen came in for a lot of teasing for her new-found love of the environment, but she put up with it very well, content in the knowledge that they now had half of the treasure clues, even if they hadn't solved any of it yet.

As soon as the buses had left for Dundalk, Judith led the helpers over to the back of the stage, where Sr Patrick, a diminutive nun, was bustling around. She greeted them cheerfully, explaining what she wanted done, as she unlocked the greenroom door.

"I asked Bradley to put up trestle tables in the corridor there," she told them, "and I have marked where each article is to go on the tables, as we take them out of the presses. It will be much easier that way."

They were hardly in the greenroom when Monica, Gwendoline and another third year,

Rachel Quinn, arrived offering their services. Sr Patrick was very pleased.

"You three can help me empty the presses," she said, "while Aileen, Nuala, Judith and Natalie can carry out those baskets there. Two girls to each basket, mind, they're heavy."

The baskets in question, about a dozen of them, were very large and of the wicker variety.

"Phew, that was heavy. I wonder what's in it," panted Judith, putting down her side of the basket and resting for a moment. Nuala lifted the lid and peered in.

"Wigs, lots of wigs and hats," she informed Judith.

"Come on, girls," called Sr Patrick. "Clothes first, then we'll clear the baskets."

A few minutes later she was called away to the phone. "Just keep on sorting," she instructed as she hurried out of the door. "I won't be long."

At first the girls diligently sorted, and the piles on the tables got higher and higher. Suddenly Nuala opened the basket which she had looked into earlier on. She rooted around and pulled out a floppy hat and also a black velvet mask which she couldn't resist.

"What do you think, chucks?" she cried, looking at herself in the long mirror. Then she picked a cloak out of one of the piles on the table, and threw it around herself. Pulling the brim of the hat low, she swaggered around. "If only I had a sword," she said, "I could be Zorro and defend the rights of the persecuted girls of St Brigid's."

Judith laughed at the sight of Nuala's masked face under the great floppy hat, its long plumes drooping down the side of her face. Then she looked at the dirndl skirt she was holding. Next minute she had it on, with its embroidered waistcoat and she rooted around for more of the costume.

"I know the exact wig for you!" cried Nuala, throwing back the lid of the basket and producing a wig with long black plaits. Judith put it on and everyone thought that she looked just like Maria in *The Sound of Music*.

Sr Patrick returned to find a medley of characters wandering around, including a cardinal, a couple of shepherds and two ladies simpering in poudré wigs and rather ancient ballgowns.

Fortunately she was amused rather than annoyed at the spectacle. Nobody had heard her return, so they all got quite a shock at the sound of her laughter in the doorway. There was a scramble to get out of the borrowed finery as quickly as possible.

"There must be at least six wigs with black plaits here," Nuala informed the nun as she slipped Judith's wig and her hat into the basket. "I never knew we had so much stuff. I thought we usually hired costumes for school plays."

"We do, because we wouldn't have enough for the large cast of a musical, for instance," replied Sr Patrick, "but we should be able to manage for smaller productions. After today at least I'll know what we do have."

It was time to get back to work. Everyone set to with a will and by the time the tea bell rang, everything was done. Sr Patrick, holding in her hand the list of contents which Judith had written down, looked around the perfectly neat and tidy room.

"You've done a wonderful job, girls," she said warmly. "I'm really grateful to you, especially for giving up your half-day to do it. Anyway, Sr Gobnait and I thought you should have some reward and we got this for you." With that she produced a box of Black Magic chocolates and handed them to Judith.

"Oh thank you, sister," Judith exclaimed as she tore off the wrappings and handed the sweets around.

"It nearly makes me sorry that I gave up art in second year," joked Nuala as the seven of them walked along to the locker room chewing contentedly.

"I don't know about that," replied Gwendoline a trifle thickly. "Sr Patrick can get terribly mad in class."

"That's true," agreed Judith. "She spits flames all around her like a mini fire-dragon."

"In that case," commented Nuala, "I'll stick to Mr Lynch who merely bangs the table and shouts a bit when I sing badly."

14

Gwendoline Saves the Day

What a ghastly place school is, thought Natalie dejectedly. She watched Miss Lawless, their Maths teacher, write on the board, "£2,500 borrowed at 9% compound interest, £1000 to be paid back each year. What is the amount owed after two years?" Natalie's dark sombre eyes looked unseeingly at the sum. Who cares, she thought, her mind drifting back to how boringly dull it was. Not for the first time she wished her mother had not been panicked into sending her to St Brigid's. The girls were nice in their way, but so unsophisticated and out of things. What did they know of weekends in London, super hotels, holidays all over the Mediterranean, parties, shopping trips, life . . . ? She caught sight of Monica at the next desk, who was so intent on the lesson that she was mouthing each sentence silently after the teacher, a strained look on her face. Perhaps her mother had been right after all, Natalie mused. Nobody would look for her, N Frossart, in a school like this.

She became aware of the teacher saying, "As you can see, the amount owed after two years comes to

£880.25." It came as quite a shock as she must have missed the whole lesson, especially when Miss Lawless finished with "Study page 94 tonight, please. Numbers 1-5."

Some time later, as they waited for the next teacher to arrive, Monica confided in Gwendoline beside her, "I'm just hopeless at compound interest. You'll have to give me a hand tonight."

"Me!" screeched Gwendoline. "You must be joking! Ask Nuala – no, Judith – she is very good at Maths."

Natalie made a mental note to ask Judith to help her at study too. Then for some reason she shivered involuntarily as she remembered Nuala's story about the woman in pink.

Everyone was sitting down eating their dinner before Nuala arrived in the refectory and slipped into her place beside Judith.

"What kept you?" asked Aileen as she passed her the salt.

"Miss Ryan, actually. She wanted me to take an urgent letter to Sr Gobnait," replied Nuala, starting to eat her dinner. "Oh no, not mince again!"

"Third time this week," Judith pointed out. "We should hold a protest meeting."

"Why didn't she give Sr Gobnait the letter herself?" persisted Aileen. "The school isn't that big."

Nuala looked at Aileen in amazement. "Since when did teachers tell mere third years their reasons for doing things?" she asked. "Though I must admit she did mutter something about being in a great rush for Dublin to get the history essays into the competition in time."

"Well," replied Aileen in a sarcastic voice, "that relieves my mind of a great worry, considering what she said about my essay yesterday."

Nuala grinned at her. "I thought it might. Anyway when I gave Sr Gobnait the letter she was so busy telling Sr Imelda something, she didn't notice me for ages and so I was late for dinner."

"Don't forget, Judith and Nuala, that we have a date on the tennis courts after school," Josie reminded them. "We're going to smash the pair of you, aren't we, Natalie?"

"Definitely," responded Natalie, cheering up. Tennis was the only thing she enjoyed in school.

"Not until after *Together and Apart*," pronounced Judith firmly. "I'm just dying to find out whether Melissa will ditch Jason for Grant or not."

Josie laughed. "I'd forgotten about that. It's a funny time to have *Together and Apart* on, isn't it?"

"The soccer international is the reason," replied Aileen. "I never realised before that you were a couch potato, Judith."

"Oh, I like to vegetate occasionally," answered Judith serenely, "but don't think I can't play a demon game of tennis, so beware."

"That's the spirit, Judith," encouraged Nuala. "I feel the same. It must be all that mince we've eaten this week."

"Someone will have to tell Sr Rosario that we'd like a change," suggested Fidelma as they all got up to leave after dinner.

116

"Good idea," responded Nuala. "Gráinne, as class captain, you are hereby elected to have the honour of speaking to the good sister about improving our menu."

"Fat chance," was Gráinne's somewhat inelegant reply. "Try some other sucker. You can bet Sr Gobnait is behind it anyway," and she ran up the stairs.

"What a cheat!" was Judith's disappointed cry later on that afternoon, when the eagerly awaited *Together and Apart* was fading from their screen.

"Imagine bringing in Jason's twin brother, that nobody had ever heard of before. He wasn't even mentioned once, ever."

"Especially when Melissa fancies him at first glance and ditches both Jason and Grant for him," grumbled Eithne. "It's just crazy."

"You can't really blame Melissa," Deirdre defended her hotly. "They are identical twins. She can't help herself."

"She's a stupid twit, ditching a perfectly nice guy like Grant for a creep like Wayne," retorted Eithne crossly. "I don't know why I bother watching."

Foolishly Nuala tried to cheer them up by joking, "Soaps are like that, probably tomorrow Melissa's cousin Noeleen will turn up and you'll find that Wayne's mother either adopted her or found her in a bin and then she forgot to tell Wayne, Jason or their father a thing about it for about twenty years at least. Don't take it too seriously."

"Everything's a joke to you, isn't it, Nuala?" hissed Deirdre. Nuala recoiled at the look on

117

Judith's and Eithne's faces.

At this point the door of the room burst open and a white-faced Gwendoline rushed in panting. She closed the door and leaned against it. "Nuala, everybody!" she cried hoarsely. "Quick, do something quickly."

"What's the matter, what's happened?" asked Nuala anxiously.

"Tell us, Gwendoline," called Judith echoed by Eithne, the trials of *Together and Apart* wiped from their minds. Gwendoline took a deep breath.

"I heard that Sr Imelda was showing two people around the school, prospective parents I suppose. I didn't pay much attention until I saw them coming up here to see the common room."

"Why? The place is fairly respectable," said Nuala thoroughly mystified.

"It's the man, he could be Natalie's cousin. He looks like an Arab and I heard him say his name was something Fatah and that they had flown from Paris to see St Brigid's."

Nuala looked hastily around the common room.

"Quick! Judith and Aileen, give me a hand with that second press," and she rushed over to where it stood crammed with books, games and various objects belonging to the third years.

Nuala cleared out the shelf of the press by simply dragging its contents out and spilling them all over the floor.

"Come on, Natalie, just to be on the safe side. If you'll scrunch up in there you'll fit. The rest of you start tidying like mad."

To their surprise Natalie made no demur, but swiftly squeezed herself into the shelf which Nuala had indicated. Nuala gathered up Natalie's long black hair and shoved it in well out of sight, then she closed the door.

"I'll leave it slightly open so that you can breathe," she explained to the hidden girl. Then she turned to the others and swiftly set the scene.

"You did say, Gwendoline, that Sr Imelda was taking them around?"

Gwendoline had barely nodded her head in assent when the door of the room opened and the nun in question entered followed by a fashionably dressed woman and a man who was unquestionably foreign-looking.

"Good afternoon, girls!" Sr Imelda greeted them with a bright smile. "Please excuse us interrupting your recreation, but I wish to show this lady and gentlemen your common room."

She looked slightly puzzled at the unusual spectacle of Aileen, Josie and Deirdre neatly stacking what appeared to be the contents of the room's presses, up against the door of the last press, which Gwendoline was carefully dusting at the same time, with her handkerchief. Her puzzlement grew when she noticed Judith busily sketching the view of the river not by the window as one would expect, but from a position which cut off access from the aforementioned presses.

The television was blaring out Advanced Physics which Eithne seemed to be totally captivated by, while Nuala was reading the first book she could snatch up – *Renaissance and Reformation* – fortunately nobody noticed she was holding it upside down.

They all turned around at the sound of the nun's voice. Nuala and Eithne stood up respectfully, while the latter turned down the television to everyone's great relief. Judith froze, as she noticed out of the corner of her eye, a long tress of black hair escaping from the underneath the press door.

"You all seem to be very busy," commented the woman pleasantly. "I like to see girls occupied." She looked at the nun as she spoke. Nuala's attention was caught by the sound of her voice, but she was distracted by the man asking in harsh tones, "What do you keep in those presses over there?"

A deadly silence hung in the air, Nuala jerked her arm nervously, inadvertently knocking her vox watch, instantly an attractive male voice announced, "It is four forty PM, it is four forty PM."

This startled the woman into looking around at Nuala who, recognising her large grey eyes, could only look back in disbelief.

"You have a lovely school here, Sister. I am sure Naomi, oh I mean Natasha would love it." The woman spoke hastily and taking the man's hand added, "Come on, darling, we must go now. Remember, we've a plane to catch."

She bundled him out of the room followed by poor Sr Imelda who couldn't understand what had caused their sudden desire to rush away.

There was silence in the room after they left. Nuala whispered to Natalie not to come out until they were sure the strangers had gone. Gwendoline suggested that she should go after them and watch them depart to be on the safe side. Nuala thankfully agreed, and Gwendoline slipped out of the room.

She wasn't long away before she returned with the good news that she had seen the couple drive off in a very large white car. Only then was the unfortunate Natalie sprung from the press.

"Poor Natalie, you must be stiff and cramped," Nuala sympathised.

Natalie stretched and groaned. "It was bad enough squeezed into such a small place, but the thing sticking into my neck was agony. It felt just like a rock or a stone and I couldn't move to get at it."

Josie ran over to the press and searched the shelf. She gave a triumphant shout and held up a crushed-looking object. "This must be it," she said.

"My missing purse!" screamed Gwendoline thankfully as she rushed over to take it from Josie. "Don't you remember I lost it? The prize money was in it. I must have thrown it in the press that day when we heard Gobnait was coming." She opened the bag and poured out a stream of one-pound coins into Aileen's hand.

"Your prize money," she said proudly.

"Yippee!" replied Aileen happily. "Now I must find Fidelma," and she rushed out of the room excitedly.

"Was he your cousin, Natalie?" asked Judith with interest reminding them all of the experience which they had just passed through.

"I don't know," confessed Natalie. "I couldn't see a thing from the press."

"I don't know who the man was," Nuala said in a serious voice, "but I recognised the woman. They must be getting desperate. She got a shock when she saw me too. That's why she rushed him out of the room."

"The woman in pink!" gasped Josie. "So she's still around. I nearly died when he asked what we kept in the presses."

"So did I, especially as I could see a long bit of Natalie's hair sticking out of one of the presses in question," agreed Judith.

"We must go and tell Sr Gobnait at once," said Nuala firmly. Gwendoline shook her head.

"We can't," she said simply. "She's gone away again for a few days."

Nuala was about to express herself freely on Sr Gobnait's selfishness at going away again, just when needed, when she noticed the frightened expression on Natalie's face.

"Don't worry, Natalie," she said bracingly. "We will look after you until Sr Gobberlets returns. Won't we, chucks?"

There was an immediate chorus of agreement from the others, who found the whole idea romantic and exciting.

Natalie's face crumpled up. "You are so kind but what could schoolgirls do to protect me? I wish Sr Gobnait hadn't gone away. She shouldn't have done so!" she said indignantly.

"Don't be silly Natalie, of course we'll be able to help you, but first of all, you'll have to have your hair cut. It sticks out a mile," replied Nuala.

"Cut off my beautiful hair? No, no!" cried Natalie, retreating away from them. "My mother would have a fit if I even thought of such a thing. She's very proud of my hair."

"Your mother would have a bigger fit if you were kidnapped," said Nuala sternly. "But suit yourself, I don't mind."

"I'll cut it for you," offered Judith. "I often cut my cousins' hair for them."

"She does," agreed Eithne. "She's not bad. Anyway remember, it'll soon grow again."

"It will grow again," said Natalie thoughtfully. "I suppose it's the best thing to do, especially as I would like to foil my cousins. They have a great cheek to try and kidnap me."

"That's the spirit!" cheered Nuala. "We'll do it tonight in the dorm after the lights are out, OK?"

Everyone agreed that it would be the best time.

"We'd better start tidying up," said Judith picking up a pile of books and opening the press doors. They all followed suit and had the room more or less in order when the bell rang.

"It will be a nice surprise for Sr Gobnait," joked Nuala.

"Our tennis match," wailed Josie "we never had it in the end."

"There's always tomorrow," consoled Judith as they all trooped off to their meal, feeling that they had really earned their tea.

15

A Hairy Incident

It was only when they were all walking over to the science lab late on the following morning that Nuala voiced a fear that had haunted her most of the night. "I was terrified there would be a row when it was discovered that Natalie had cut her hair," she confessed to Judith, "but very few people seem to have even noticed it."

Judith looked at Natalie walking ahead of them, deep in conversation with Gwendoline. Since Natalie had realised that it was really Gwendoline who had saved her from being located by her cousins, she had made a point of seeking her company. They were now discovering they had a lot in common.

"It occurred to me too, especially as I had done the cutting," Judith replied. "I suppose it isn't so noticeable because as soon as it was shortened, the rest of her hair went all wavy and bushy. She doesn't seem to stick out of the crowd so much either, did you notice?"

"You made a brilliant job of it," said Nuala loyally. "You'll never be stuck for a job!"

They both laughed at the thought of Judith looking for a job. By this time they had reached the lab door. As they went in they could hear Gráinne commenting, "There's something different about you today, Natalie, isn't there, Rachel?" She appealed to another of the class standing beside her.

Rachel gave Natalie a long appraising look.

"It's her hair I think," she replied at last. "You're doing it another way, it looks a lot better."

Gwendoline, who had been listening to this interchange with nervous interest, rushed in with, "I think Natalie's hair looks really brilliant that way."

Nuala smiled at Judith and murmured, "You see what I mean . . . "

Judith grinned back at her in return. "Thank goodness for that."

Science class was nearly over and most people were cleaning away their part of the bench, when Gráinne asked Miss Crilly about the next outing of Boynepeace.

"It will be on Thursday to Monasterboice," replied the teacher. "As it's at least ten miles from here, you'll be travelling by coach. Please remember that you're representing St Brigid's and behave yourselves there." She glanced keenly around the laboratory making some girls feel guilty quite unnecessarily.

"Aren't you coming with us too?" asked Deirdre.

"No, Miss Ryan is taking you there. It's really a history outing. In fact I think she intends devoting class this afternoon to it," was the teacher's reply.

As they were walking back to the castle, Eithne who had been one of the first to leave the lab, came out of the locker room looking mysterious and crooked her finger at Nuala, Josie and Aileen.

"Come in here," she whispered. "I've something to show you."

Quickly following her into the room they found Fidelma cradling something in her arms wrapped in crisp white tissue paper. Eithne carefully peeled the top layer of the tissue back revealing a very long plait of glossy black hair, tied with narrow ribbon top and bottom.

"Natalie's hair," she announced proudly. "When Judith cut it off we rescued it and prepared it for her, just in case her mother has a fit when she sees her short hair. It's well done isn't it?"

"Brilliant!" replied the astounded Nuala. "Where did you get such super tissue paper?"

"Gwendoline, of course. She always has loads of it. In fact she was the one who suggested using it."

Judith looked at her cousins and commented, "What an extraordinary pair you are. Imagine thinking of such a thing!"

"I think it's a great idea," observed Aileen. "She can always clip it to her head and drop it over one shoulder. It would fool her mother, until she had time to break the news to her anyway."

Nuala looked keenly at Aileen, saying slowly, "That's given me an idea for Monasterboice on Thursday. That cousin may turn up again with his pink friend."

"Surely not! They must have given up by now," protested Eithne.

"You're probably right, but better safe than sorry," replied Nuala. "I'll have to check something first. I'll let you all know later if it goes well."

Immediately after school was over, Nuala disappeared and wasn't seen again until tea time. She came into the refectory then and sat down at her place, looking pleased about something.

"Sr Imelda has given me permission to speak to the whole year privately for five minutes at the beginning of study," she said demurely, handing her plate up to Monica who was serving that evening.

Many and varied were the questions that were fired at her from all sides in response to this announcement, but Nuala refused to give any further information, except to say, "Wait and see."

When Sr Imelda arrived five minutes late, as promised, to take study that evening, she was intrigued by the sound of excited laughter coming from the study room. It was third years' reply to Nuala's last remark: "Does everyone understand what to do if I call Red Alert?"

The weather, which had suddenly become dull and showery the previous week, decided on Thursday to surprise everyone with a warm sunny morning for a change.

In consequence on the morning in question, the coach drove off to Monasterboice with everyone on board in great form and carrying quite a few cameras between them.

As they passed out of the coach and through the gateway of Monasterboice they discovered that the place was free of visitors apart from themselves.

After a short talk from Miss Ryan, they wandered around in the sun and admired the round tower and high crosses there, especially the famous High Cross of Muiredach, which the teacher had just told them was one of the most perfect examples of a high cross in Ireland.

"It's really a graveyard," Natalie pointed out, as she looked at the tombstones surrounding them.

"True," agreed Judith, "but it's not scary especially with the sun shining on everything."

"It has an unbelievably peaceful atmosphere" observed Josie. "As if nothing bad had ever happened here."

"Which is strange, considering its history," replied Nuala. "But I know what you mean, there is something timeless and peaceful about this place."

Aileen had gone off looking for clue number three, atmospheres weren't things she paid much attention too.

Gwendoline had brought her camera with her, determined to photograph everything of note. Having done that she was looking rather disconsolately around her when she caught sight of Natalie and a few others looking up at the famous round tower. She pointed to a short flight of steps which led up to the locked door of this tower.

"Natalie, go and stand on the steps, I want to take a photograph of you," she called over.

Natalie was only too happy to oblige, then

Gwendoline took some of Monica, Gráinne and Rachel with and without Natalie, then Monica suggested that Gwendoline should be included in the next photograph.

Nuala, who happened to be near by, offered to take these photographs so Gwendoline handed over her expensive Canon camera, with some hasty instructions, before she took her place on the top step above her friends.

When Nuala had finished taking the photographs, Natalie, Monica and Rachel ran down the steps together. Gwendoline was about to follow them when a sudden beam of fractured light beyond the boundary wall caught her attention. Her curiosity aroused, she stood on tiptoe and leant against the tower. She looked across at the place where she thought that she had seen the light.

At first she could see only fields and trees, then as she watched, a large white car backed very slowly up a narrow laneway between the fields and stopped there. It must have been the sun reflecting on the car's windscreen she thought as she ran down the steps to where Nuala was waiting to hand back the precious camera.

Just as she reached Nuala it suddenly struck Gwendoline that she had seen that particular car before.

"Nuala!" she cried. "There's a big white car parked in the laneway across from here. It looks exactly like the one Natalie's cousin drove away in that day."

Nuala's eyes widened. "I thought as much," she replied with satisfaction.

"You think it's them again?" asked Gwendoline.

"I do. Pass the word around," Nuala ordered crisply. "It's Red Alert time."

Within minutes, five girls carrying black plastic bags could be seen slipping out of sight behind the round tower, while Gráinne and Deirdre went over to Miss Ryan and asked her to come with them to look at some very weird gravestone which they had just discovered.

While this was going on in Monasterboice itself, the driver of the white car in the laneway took a pair of powerful binoculars out of her capacious handbag and spoke to the man beside her.

"I suppose the girls are all in there, looking at the round tower. This is a perfect place to watch them as they come out and get into that coach. If your cousin's one of them there is no way she can escape me seeing her."

She raised the binoculars and looking through them scanned the area around them. It wasn't long before she gave a pleased exclamation.

"Aha!" she cried. "Here's the first of them coming out of the gate." After a pause her companion heard her say, "That's funny, very funny."

"What's funny, Annaliese?" grunted the man impatiently.

"I saw a girl in the first group that was getting into the coach. I was sure it was your cousin Natalie, she was very tanned-looking with the famous long black hair hanging to one side, but when I looked more closely she didn't look a bit like the one in the photograph," she replied without taking her eyes off the schoolgirls walking in groups towards the waiting coach.

A tense few minutes passed then she cried again. "Wait, here's another one."

The man watched her eagerly. However it soon became apparent from her expression that once again the girl wasn't his cousin either.

When Annaliese had seen the last third year followed by the teacher climb up into the coach she flung her binoculars roughly into the back of her car and raged through gritted teeth. "I'm baffled, completely baffled, I counted five girls who could have passed themselves off as your wretched cousin Natalie. Imagine five girls in one class . . . You don't think those brats are up to something, do you? I wonder . . ." Tearing down the photograph of Natalie which had been propped against the windscreen, she ripped it to pieces. Then she opened the car door.

"What are you doing, where are you going?" demanded the startled man in a harsh voice.

Annaliese swung herself out of the car, showing a lot of plump leg in the process. "I am going to interview the teacher in that coach. Don't worry about her recognising me," she hissed haughtily back at him. "I'll tell her a little story and when she sees who I am, she'll accept it without question. Only a short time ago I told one of my stories in court and the judge said that he was confident that my version of the event was undoubtedly the correct one. He had no hesitation in accepting it and gave me good expenses, etc. Snobby little man." Laughing nastily she slammed the car door, and strode confidently down the lane.

She turned into the road just in time to see the St Brigid's coach come swiftly down towards her. She stepped hastily back but not in time to avoid the huge splashes of cold muddy water thrown up by the wheels of the coach as it passed through one of the myriad pools in its path, a result of the previous week's weather. Mahmoud, who had followed her morosely down the lane, saw the whole incident, which made him to look happy for the first time in weeks.

"That will cost you an extra five thousand pounds!" shrieked Annaliese, hastily mopping her face and neck with a tissue as she rejoined him.

"Five thousand?" he echoed in surprise.

"Yes, five thousand pounds," she enunciated. "Remember I'm only obliging you because Perdita had to give up. She thought that one of the girls in the school might have connected her with the time she was in the museum. Another thing I'll have you know is that I'm not in the habit of driving people around. In my career I'm used to chauffeur-driven cars. So if you want me to go on helping you to find your cousin you've got to pay for it and I'm not even charging you for my time at that!"

Mahmoud looked disdainfully at her. "You'll get

your money when we find the girl. I do not haggle with women." He spoke contemptuously. They returned to the car in silence.

"Where now?" she asked unpleasantly as she turned on the ignition.

"Dublin," he replied shortly. "There's no point in wasting any more time here."

Back at St Brigid's the third years found it hard to settle down after their exciting morning. Natalie thanked them over and over again.

"There's no need to thank us," protested Nuala. "We all enjoyed fooling them."

"Yes," agreed Judith. "It was great fun. It made the outing to Monasterboice even better" – a sentiment that reflected accurately the feelings of everybody present.

"By the way, Nuala, what story did you tell Sr Patrick to get the wigs from her?" asked Eithne.

"The truth really. I just said we wanted to hoax somebody by pretending to be Natalie," replied Nuala. "She thought it was a great joke. The only thing I'm sorry about is that we've missed the third clue."

"The third clue!" cried Josie. "We forgot all about it. We'll never work out the puzzle without it."

Aileen gave a yelp and then smiled complacently.

"Just as well some people keep their minds on the essentials," she pronounced primly, producing a folded piece of paper from her pocket. "I found this tied to the rail on the steps of the round tower. It had 'Wet Paint' written on the outside but when I opened it, it had the usual stuff written on the inside. When you called Red Alert, Nuala, I stuffed it in my pocket and forgot all about it until this minute."

She unfolded the piece of paper and passed it to Nuala who read it out slowly. "'MDCXII'– that's one thousand and – what's 'D'?"

"500," called Gráinne.

"That's 1500 plus 112 equals 1612, isn't that right?" asked Nuala.

Everyone thought.

"1612 is right," replied Judith.

16

The Happy Traveller

Sharon Kennedy looked around the crowded grill room of the *Happy Traveller*, a new roadhouse some miles from Drogheda.

"I like this place, Mum," she pronounced approvingly. "Isn't the food super, Lisa? Though I suppose anything would be, after the rubbish they give us to eat at school."

"The food is just out of this world," replied her friend Lisa, sitting beside her. "It was brilliant of you asking me out today like this, Mrs Kennedy."

"It's the best place for miles, you know," said Mrs Kennedy, smiling complacently. "We love having you, Lisa. Had you two any trouble getting out of St Brigid's today?"

Sharon laughed. "Not us! Sr Gobnait is away until this evening and Sr Imelda just eats out of my hand, doesn't she, Lisa?" Her voice, clearly audible above the chatting buzz of the grill room, carried to the table behind them where a morose couple were silently eating their lunch.

"She certainly does," chuckled Lisa. "Remember we have to be back for study though."

"The Leaving Cert mocks are on this week," explained Sharon. "That normally wouldn't affect us, but there's a rumour going around that the silly old crow Gobnait is thinking of making us all do mid-term tests as well. She has a down on us fifth years, says we only think of clothes and make-up."

Her mother frowned slightly at the disrespectful way she spoke of Sr Gobnait while Lisa giggled and nodded in agreement. "I don't think that you should call Sr Gobnait a silly old crow," Mrs Kennedy reproved, but mildly, Sharon being almost perfect in her eyes.

"Well, I only called her that because I don't want to shock you, Mum, with what we *really* call her," Sharon retorted defiantly, tossing her head in annoyance. "She is more than that, I can tell you. If you heard the telling-off she gave me the other day because I merely requested Judith O'Brien and that Natalie something-or-other to clear off the tennis courts and make room for a few of us fifth years, you'd call her a much worse name."

"It's true Mrs Kennedy," agreed Lisa solemnly. "The third years are terribly cheeky this year, especially Nuala O'Donnell and her crowd. I've noticed they've taken up this Natalie as well."

"You should see her, Mum. She wears her long black hair in an affected way over one shoulder, has huge eyes in what you could only call a dark brown face and goes around the place as if she owned it."

Mrs Kennedy was intrigued. "A foreigner then, where's she from?" she asked.

"She's supposed to come from Scotland," Sharon's voice was heavily sarcastic. "Scotland, I ask you – with a face like that!"

"She is a real mystery kid," commented Lisa, "who arrived late in the summer term out of the blue looking different to everyone else. Last night Orla heard one of the sixth years asking the head girl was it true that Natalie was wanted by the police. Mary shut her up so quickly that it made – her wonder was there any truth in it."

Before Sharon or her mother who had been listening with great interest could join in wondering was there anything in it too, a waiter appeared beside their table. He was accompanied by a trolley laden with such a mouth-watering selection of desserts that Natalie was quite forgotten in the more important matter of making their choice from amongst them.

The couple at the table behind them were still silent but looked happier then before. The woman ordered more coffee. When it came they sipped it slowly as they listened intently to Sharon holding forth on St Brigid's and the difficulties of getting out again to go to a fashion show with her mother.

"If the rumour is true," she was saying in a complaining voice, "and there's mid-term tests for the rest of us, we'll all be stuck inside most of next week. The sixth years go home for a long weekend, but there's no talk of us getting even a half-day."

"We might," Lisa pointed out. "The juniors, that is up to and including third years, are having one of those Boynepeace outings so that'll leave us

137

fifth years and she might give us the half-day then."

"What's Boynepeace?" asked Mrs Kennedy, diverted by the name.

"It's a sort of club, they go on outings to monuments and rave about the environment," replied Sharon impatiently, displaying her lack of interest in the subject.

"It sounds green, which is all the rage now. I'm very green myself," stated her mother firmly.

"You should meet Miss Crilly," Lisa said to Mrs Kennedy. "Now she's really nuts on the environment. We have a special place in the school grounds, you know. It's called Calfe's Pool."

"That's where Boynepeace is going next Thursday," Sharon offered the information sulkily. "Miss Crilly came into the office when I was there this morning and told Sr Imelda. I think she's cracked."

Mrs Kennedy tittered and put down her coffee cup. "I think we'd better go, girls, if we want a good peek at the shops. I must have you back in time for study. I don't want to annoy Sr Gobnait, she mixes with top people you know." Noticing the surprised look on Lisa's face, she added kindly, "The Minister for Education, dear."

She called for her bill and a few minutes later the whole party left in a flutter of scarves and jackets.

"Did you hear that?" asked the man at the next table. "Good thing we stopped here for lunch."

"I heard it all. Leave it to me. I'm an expert at finding out things," his companion replied confidently. "Don't worry, we'll soon have that little bird in our hands. I promise."

"You'd better be right. I'm getting impatient," he grunted as he rose from the table. The excellent meal he had just consumed, plus the good news about Natalie being at St Brigid's, mellowed him sufficiently to leave a generous tip, surprising the waiter who hadn't expected anything from such a surly couple.

That evening Sharon and Lisa were delayed by heavy traffic on their return journey to school. Luckily they managed to slip unobtrusively into the hall as study was commencing particularly as Sr Gobnait made an appearance there only about five minutes later.

"I am sorry to disturb you, girls," she apologised "but I wanted to warn third and fifth years that we decided at the staff meeting this afternoon to give the mid-term tests next week, when the Leaving and Group Cert mocks are on. However you will be glad to hear that there will be a half-day for both years on Friday."

Lisa looked significantly at Sharon at the next desk. "It seems as if rumour was right for once," she murmured as Sr Gobnait left the room.

"You're right," Sharon agreed. "And do you realise that we'll be able to go to that fashion show? I'll ring Mum tomorrow."

17

Fakes and Fishing Rods

"What did you think of the Maths?" Judith asked Nuala and Aileen as they walked back from their classroom after the last mid-term test.

"It was a horror," stated Aileen frankly. "I hope my parents haven't any ambitions about me becoming a nuclear physicist or an accountant because if they have, they're in for a big disappointment."

Judith laughed. "I don't suppose the thought has crossed their minds," she replied.

"Anyway, the mouldy old tests are over now. Let's forget them," suggested Nuala, "and concentrate on this afternoon at Calfe's Pool. The sun is shining and the last clue is beckoning to us."

"Are you talking about the treasure?" asked Gwendoline as she and Natalie joined them. "I would simply love to find the last clue, especially as I got Mummy to send me a book on breaking codes. I thought it might come in useful."

"You're an asset to the class, Gwendoline," shouted Nuala over the din in the corridor, cluttered with girls pouring out of classrooms on their way to dinner. "A book on codes is a brilliant idea. When we get the last clue we'll all get together and hammer out the solution."

As soon as dinner was over the class in twos and threes walked through the grounds to where Miss Crilly was waiting for them beside the river. It was very pleasant there with the lush greenery around them, and the sun sparkling on the water. They grouped themselves around her for the usual preliminary talk. She had hardly repeated the Boynepeace motto of 'Recycle, Reuse and Refill' when there was an unexpected interruption.

Nobody had noticed the approach of a white car, but suddenly a woman, dressed smartly in navy, appeared out of one, requesting urgent speech with the teacher. Miss Crilly frowned at this unforeseen intrusion but acquiesced to the stranger's request with courtesy. The two women spoke quietly together, then Miss Crilly called Natalie over to her.

"This lady," she explained, "has a letter for you from your mother, she says. Perhaps you should read it."

As Natalie moved towards the newcomer, Nuala, Gwendoline and Judith automatically accompanied her.

"My mother," gasped Natalie. "There's nothing wrong with her is there?" She almost snatched the letter from the woman's hand and tore it open.

"Not a thing," replied the woman. "She's very well. Just read what she has written."

She exchanged an understanding glance with

Miss Crilly. Nuala took stock of the stranger as Natalie read the letter. Though she had never seen her before, there was something about her which seemed faintly familiar.

Then Natalie turned to Nuala and silently handed her the letter, an anxious questioning look on her face. So Nuala, with Judith and Gwendoline peering over her shoulder, opened it and read:

> *"My Darling Natalie,*
>
> *You may remember your grandfather's secretary Perdita Remor, this is her sister, Annaliese, who has offered to go and bring you home. There is no longer any need for you to hide out in St Brigid's. I have written to Sr Gobnait about it too.*
>
> *Longing to see you soon.*
>
> *My dearest love,*
>
> > > *Mum x x x x"*

"Is that your mother's handwriting?" asked Nuala briskly.

Natalie nodded.

"I'm surprised Sr Gobnait didn't come with it herself," Nuala commented. "It's not like her." She looked over at the stranger as she spoke and was startled to see a pair of rather protuberant eyes looking angrily at her.

"I am taking Natalie up to Sr Gobnait, of course. She has to collect her clothes too. It's quicker by car," the stranger snapped back at her.

Miss Crilly relaxed. "Oh, you're going back to the school then," she remarked in a relieved voice.

The strange woman smiled tolerantly at her. "Of course. You're right to be careful though. I can understand that. You have such a great responsibility being in charge of so many young girls . . ." Her voice was smooth and understanding.

Miss Crilly was plainly impressed. "You'd better go Natalie," she said kindly. Natalie said goodbye to everyone in turn and was especially affectionate to Nuala and Gwendoline.

"We'll keep in touch," they promised her. She nodded speechlessly in return. Everyone was plainly affected.

The woman got into the driving seat of the car, while Natalie gave one last vigorous wave to the watching girls. Then she got into the seat beside the driver.

As the car moved slowly away Miss Crilly called briskly, "Come along girls, we've wasted enough time already."

Everyone turned reluctantly away and walked slowly behind the teacher, back to the riverbank. They hadn't even reached it when the air was suddenly rent by a series of piercing screams. Immediately everyone swung around again, and stared in amazement at the scene before them.

The white car which they had watched drive away was now parked beside a group of trees, just before the road disappeared from their view in the woods. Natalie was struggling to get away from a man, who was plainly trying to push her back into the car.

As they stood frozen by this extraordinary

143

spectacle they heard Natalie scream, "Help! Oh please help!" spurring Nuala, Judith and Aileen into action. They ran towards the car but before they reached it something with a hissing sound snaked out swiftly from amongst the trees towards the man. He gave a terrible scream and clapped both hands to his neck and shoulder, thereby releasing Natalie.

She ran immediately over to her friends. "It's Mahmoud, my cousin Mahmoud!" she panted, holding fast to Nuala and Aileen who had reached her first.

Mahmoud was now kneeling on the ground writhing and moaning. As they watched, fascinated, a man appeared from the trees, a gun in one hand, a fishing-rod in the other. He walked over to Mahmoud and stuck the gun in his back.

"Stop struggling, you're only making things worse," he commanded in a loud voice.

Nuala stared at the mild face complete with glasses. "Why," she cried at last, "it's Professor Jenkins. What's he doing here?"

The professor dropped his fishing-rod and raised his battered hat. "Good afternoon, ladies. I seem to have caught a fish at last," he replied in a satisfied voice.

Just then another car drove up and out jumped Steve the tennis coach.

"Hang on, Percy, I'll take over now," he shouted as he joined the Professor. "I've come prepared," and so saying he produced a black case. The two men huddled over Mahmoud.

It didn't take long to get the hook out and within minutes a hand-cuffed Mahmoud was led over to Steve's car. As soon as Mahmoud was placed in the back seat of the car a figure erupted out of the white car and flung herself on the professor.

"How can I thank you" she cooed sincerely "for rescuing us from that dreadful man?" She held out her hand. "I am a journalist with *Daily Data* and I was taking dear Natalie home to her mother when this monster attacked us. I'm so pleased to meet you."

Natalie gave a strangled yelp which died when she saw Professor Jenkins pointing the gun at the journalist.

"Annaliese Phibbs," he said sternly. "I am taking you into custody, where you will be charged with the attempted kidnap of Natalie Frossart, with your accomplice whom you have described as 'that dreadful man' or was it 'monster'?"

He pushed her over to the car and handcuffed her to Mahmoud, who looked unpleasantly at her but said nothing.

"I will be back when I've unloaded this lot," called the Professor getting into the car and waving Steve to drive on.

A great spontaneous cheer rose from the watchers who had been silent up to now. Then they all surrounded Natalie clapping her back and asking questions.

"We'd just moved off when I saw Mahmoud in the car mirror," she explained breathlessly. "He was hiding in the back, so I opened the door and jumped out, he followed me and you know the rest. I wonder who Professor Jenkins is though . . . "

Before anyone had time to answer a man came rushing from the direction of the river shouting, "Who stole my spare fishing rod? I turned my back for a moment and when I looked again it was gone. If it was one of you I'll have your guts for garters!"

"Mike Greene," called a furious voice. "How dare you . . . aah!" trailed off into a scream, followed by a large splash.

"Help!" screamed Gwendoline. "Miss Crilly has fallen into the river."

18

Consequences

"Alison!" shouted Mike Greene, as he rushed past the screaming girls, tearing off his jacket as he ran and throwing it to one side. It landed at Gwendoline's feet. Immediately she bent down and picked it up. As she did so an envelope fell out of one of its pockets.

To the delight of all, the eccentric master from Newgrange College dived fully-clothed into the Boyne to rescue their science teacher. Whether she needed rescuing was something nobody even considered.

Gráinne, with the help of Nuala, Judith and Josie, organised the class into two groups on the riverbank. Within minutes willing hands were pulling the two soaking wet teachers up and out of the river.

As Miss Crilly, spluttering, coughing and shivering, was ineffectually squeezing water from her hair and clothes, Mike draped his dry jacket, kindly handed to him by Gwendoline, around her and came to a decision.

"That white car there, we'll take it and I'll drive

you up to the school. I don't want you getting pneumonia," he declared masterfully. "Girls, tell the owner, if he comes, that it will be at the school."

Monica sighed deeply. "He's just like Kevin Costner in *The Bodyguard*, isn't he?" she breathed to Aileen standing next to her.

"I can't believe it's the same man!" retorted Aileen. "The one who keeps vats of wet paper in a shed."

"It's love, it brings out the best in us," said Nuala soulfully, teasing them. "Wait until we break the news to David and Paul, they'll never believe us."

As they were talking Miss Crilly reluctantly agreed to go in the car on the condition that Natalie accompany them.

"I'm still in a state of shock about that woman," she told Natalie. "I really believed her, and to think that all the time she was coolly kidnapping you under my very nose. I won't let you out of my sight again until I hand you over to Sr Gobnait herself."

Natalie, who was feeling very shaken as well, meekly got into the car while Miss Crilly gave instructions to the other girls about returning to school at once.

"Gráinne, as class captain, I will hold you responsible if anyone gets lost," was her parting admonition as the car moved away.

"Poor old Crillers, this whole affair has really knocked her spare," said Aileen. "Imagine thinking anyone would get lost in the school grounds."

"You'd think she would be used to adventures by now," agreed Judith. "After all the excitement of the last few terms."

"What I don't understand is how she knew we would be here today," commented Nuala who hadn't been listening to the others. "Could she have an accomplice in the school, the woman who tried to snatch Natalie I mean?"

"Oh that woman," replied Aileen. "You're right. They probably bugged the school on their last visit."

"You've something there," agreed Josie. "But I expect we'll never find out the truth now."

They were interrupted by Gwendoline who handed an envelope to Aileen. "This fell out of Mr Greene's pocket but, as your name is on it, I suppose I can give it to you."

Aileen, looking mystified, tore open the envelope and took out its contents, which she read intently, then laughed.

"It's from David, he says that they couldn't leave the clue yesterday as their outing was cancelled, but Mr Greene promised to deliver it to us, when he was fishing here today."

"Well I had hoped to find the last clue," remarked Gwendoline cheerfully, "and so I did in a way."

"We'd better hurry up," said Judith. "All the others are out of sight."

Gráinne came back looking worried. "What's keeping you lot?" she asked. "It's nearly tea time, and I don't want to be late."

"Put away the clue, we'll look at it after tea," said Nuala. "We're coming Gráinne," and breaking into a run she led the way back.

They reached the school in time to see Sr Gobnait ushering a happy-looking Mr Greene into the white car again.

"What I can't understand," the tall nun was saying, "is why would a successful woman like that do such a thing? It couldn't be for money alone, surely."

"I can't imagine, Sister," he replied cheerfully. "'Nowt so queer as folks,' as they say." He got into the car and drove away, obviously not so prejudiced against fossil fuels as his pupils had stated.

The refectory was abuzz with excitement at tea. It was hard to know which episode was of greater interest to the girls, the attempted kidnapping of Natalie or near drowning and dramatic rescue of the science teacher. Natalie wasn't present at the meal, which ensured that the conversation was unrestrained.

Sr Gobnait had taken her up to the infirmary and she was now safely in bed under the watchful eye of Sr Joseph. As there was a film on that evening in the gym, the common room was empty when Nuala, Judith and other interested parties arrived there to study the four clues which they had collected from the various sites.

Just as Nuala placed the four pieces of paper on the table and read out, "1366 – 1615 – 1915 – 1253," Gwendoline came in with the promised code-breaking book.

"What possible link could there be between these four numbers," Nuala murmured aloud, while Judith picked up the code book and flicked through it.

"Look at this!" she cried. "It's the alphabet with numbers under it, we could try that."

"What do you mean?" asked Nuala. "I don't understand."

"Look, the first number on the list is 1366, now if you take one as an A, three as a C and six as F, we get ACFF," explained Judith excitedly.

"That sounds quite hopeful. I'll help you to work out the other three," suggested Aileen producing a Biro and paper.

"Good idea," agreed Judith sitting down at the table beside her.

"We'll work on the other puzzle. I have the four pieces here, I'll just put them together," said Nuala suiting action to words, producing the following:

Whe re Fi vet Reesg Ro
Wtog Eth erin T heho llo wby
thep Ooly ouw illf in dth elon
gedf oRt Rea suRe inT hehea tHe
RSNI CEAN dcoOl

"I've looked through this book and there's nothing like that in it," complained Gwendoline.

"I'm not surprised. I don't think words like Reesg Ro, Ooly, hehea mean anything. David and Paul are just making mugs of us," said Josie, fiddling with her hair and wondering would she have time to tie it up before the film. The door opened and Sr Gobnait stood before them.

"Come along, girls!" she commanded kindly if briskly. "You should be in the gym, *Star Trek 6* is about to start."

"How is Natalie?" asked Judith as Nuala hastily gathered the pieces of puzzle paper up, stuffing them between the pages of a book.

"Natalie is fine," smiled Sr Gobnait. "She will be back for class tomorrow morning."

They all trooped out of the common room. "We can work on it in the dorm tonight," Aileen said to Judith as they were sitting in their seats waiting for the film to begin.

Judith nodded. "I'm glad we are in time for the beginning of *Star Trek 6*," she replied happily.

After lights out that night, Aileen arrived in Judith's cubicle. Sitting down on the bed she produced a piece of paper with ACFFAFAEABECAIAE written on it.

Judith struggled into a sitting position. "I can't see a thing, we need more light," she complained.

Aileen silently switched on her torch, illuminating the line of letters in front of them. "Let's see, CAAB - no CAIFF, that's not right either, what about BECAIA. It doesn't make sense," she said in a disappointed voice.

"I'll try," suggested Judith. "What about CAFFE or EIAC. No, we must be on the wrong track."

They sat in silence, looking at the letters for about five minutes completely baffled. Then Judith looked thoughtfully at Aileen and spoke slowly.

"The treasure must be in one of the places we went to, so let's see if the letters make up one of those names."

Aileen brightened up. "Take Pearlach, we have EAAC but no R or H." She looked at the numbers again: P = 16, 12 = L. "Maybe we have the sequence wrong. Back to the drawing board."

Judith said nothing but hastily wrote, '1615 = PO, 1253 = LEC, 1366 = MEE and 1915 = SO = POLECMEESO.'

"It's Carraigphooca," cried Aileen excitedly. A few sleepy voices called "Hush" and someone said, "Go to sleep, whoever you are."

"Look," whispered Aileen. "POOCA, if you change LE to AB."

"I don't know," argued Judith. "It could be Calfe's Pool that way too. 131265. It's one of them I bet."

Aileen rolled up the pages of a copybook, covered with numbers and letters. "I'd better go back to bed, we'll show it to the others in the morning and see what they think."

Judith snuggled down under her quilt again. "Good idea," she yawned. "Good night, Aileen."

Aileen slipped quietly back to her own cubicle, resisting the impulse to shine her torch over the ceiling and howl like a banshee. "That would shake them up," she chuckled to herself.

When morning came Aileen and Judith were late getting down to breakfast, so that it wasn't until mid-morning break that they had any time to discuss their doings of the night before. However, when they confronted Nuala with the result of their labours, she not only agreed with Aileen but triumphantly revealed that she had cracked the second part of the puzzle.

"It was Sr Imelda who gave me the clue," she recounted, laughing at their surprised faces and also those of Natalie, Gwendoline, Josie and the Murrays, who were all sitting on a low wall outside, enjoying the sun during their brief break-time.

"How come?" asked Josie.

"Well," explained Nuala, "if you remember we had grammar with her today and she was boring on about punctuation and capital letters. When I opened my grammar book, there in front of me was the coded message and as I looked, it clicked and all was made clear."

"I don't understand what you're talking about," complained Gwendoline, making a place for Monica who had joined them by now.

Nuala pulled out the papers from her pocket and smoothed out the creases.

"Look, there's the code. 'Whe re Fi vet Reesg Ro Wtog eth er.' Now push the words together and you get 'Where five trees grow together'!" Nuala exclaimed triumphantly.

"Yes, yes of course," agreed Judith. "The next line must be 'in the hollow by the pool'."

"'You will find the longed for treasure, in the heathers nice and cool'," Nuala finished for them.

"That's brilliant, Nuala!" exclaimed Aileen. "It's definitely Carraigphooca, there's a pool and lots of trees there."

Just then the bell rang for class and they were all arguing about it as they went back along the corridors. Both Aileen and Judith were determined to be proved right.

As soon as afternoon school was over Judith, carrying a spade borrowed from the gardener and accompanied by Josie, Monica, Eithne, Fidelma and Gwendoline complete with rubber gloves, left quietly for Calfe's Pool. About the same time Nuala and Aileen set out defiantly for Carraigphooca. The great treasure hunt was on, with both sides convinced they had the only correct solution.

19

Findings and Fortunes

Carraigphooca looked cold and remote when Nuala and Aileen reached it after twenty minutes of brisk walking. The sun which had been shining all day suddenly disappeared behind a cloud. Immediately a nasty little cold breeze with a hint of rain in it sprang up.

"It's a bit scary here, isn't it?" Aileen remarked with an involuntary shiver. "So quiet and lonely. I wonder why it's called a fairy rock?"

Nuala looked shocked. "Don't you know?" she asked. "It was like this: One day many many years ago a couple of young girls wandered here, tired out with the heat of the day, they fell asleep just about where you're standing now. They were asleep for some time when suddenly they woke up. They sat up in surprise at the sight of the moon flooding the place with its light, making it as bright as day. As they watched they noticed the big rock over there, the central one which juts out, was moving slowly, very slowly away from the others."

"Why did it move?" asked Aileen, grinning. "As

if I didn't know. Go on anyway."

"I thought you might say that. Well the next thing they saw was some brightly dressed happy little people coming out from behind the rock, singing and dancing. The pair were terrified out of their wits, especially when the little people joined hands and went sliding down the waterfall together and fell into those primroses and heathers there and literally disappeared."

"Get out the rhyme, Nuala," Aileen urged. "I don't want to be late out here in case your little fairy chums come dancing out making us witless too."

"In your case, Aileen, it would be unnecessary," retorted Nuala laughingly but she produced her notebook and read:

"Where five trees grow together
In the hollows by the pool
You will find the longed for treasure
In the heather nice and cool."

Aileen pointed her finger and screeched with excitement, "Look Nuala, there on the rocks, there's a group of little trees, overlooking a pool of water! Could it be there?"

Nuala walked over to the massive outcrop of rock. Sure enough she could see a little group of trees, young sycamores she guessed, growing out of a mossy mound of grass. Just below them was a deep pool of water in a natural fissure in the rock.

"I'll climb up and count the trees – if there are

five we'll take it that it's the right place," Nuala said, then she swiftly ran up and over the rocky ledges to the top before Aileen could answer her. "You're right – there are five trees in the group but I can't see any place where the treasure could be," she called back.

Aileen watched as Nuala started to wander around the outcrop, poking in any likely places apparently without any success. Then Nuala gave a shout, waving her arms in the air about her. Aileen's hopeful expression changed to horror though when she saw Nuala slip and tumble down the little waterfall coming to land heavily in the boggy ground beneath.

Aileen rushed over to where the inert figure of her friend lay plastered with mud. "Nuala!" she cried. "God, she's dead. What'll I do? What'll I do?"

Nuala lifted up her muddy face. "I'm alive I think," she groaned. "Though the primroses and heathers will never be the same again."

The badly shaken Aileen didn't know whether to laugh or cry. "Are you terribly hurt, Nuala?" she asked anxiously.

"No, I don't think so. This muddy patch broke my fall," Nuala answered limply. She opened her eyes again and placed her hand on the rock beside her for help in levering herself up. Aileen stretched out her hand and between that and the rock Nuala managed to get up from the boggy ground. When she was standing looking like "the beast from the swamp" as Aileen described it later, she found to her surprise a large piece of rock had come away in her hand. She looked at it and then at the rock face.

"That's funny," she remarked. "It looks as if this piece of rock was plugging that hole in the rock there." She placed the rock against the hole. It fitted perfectly. She put the rock down and rooted around in the hole. "You were right, Aileen. I must admit I had doubts about Carraigphooca," she confessed as she pulled out a bundle and handed it to the jubilant Aileen.

"I knew it was here!" cried Aileen as she examined their find. It was quite bulky and wrapped in very dark green, almost black material. "I'm just dying to see Judith and Josie's faces when they see this," gloated Aileen.

"I'm just dying to get out of this uniform and wash myself," replied Nuala, looking wryly at her mud-encrusted skirt and jumper now hardening in the wind. She started to pick the lumps of mud off her face and hands.

Aileen led the way, sneaking ahead and making sure the coast was clear for Nuala who had no desire to be seen in her bedraggled, filthy state. They were both weary when they had finally reached the haven of the dormitory.

Nuala felt exhausted, but a thorough wash and clean clothes soon restored her. As she was drying her hair Aileen came in to her cubicle carrying the precious parcel. She sat on the bed watching Nuala.

"It's a miracle you're weren't hurt," she said. "I really thought you were dead. I'm not the better of it yet."

Nuala fixed her hair, looking in the mirror. "You're not the better of it! I'll never get over it," she pronounced. "But Aileen, if we've beaten the boys, not to mention Judith and Co, I'm happy to sacrifice myself. Flick over the goods."

Aileen handed over the treasure, pressing her fingers on the coverings. "What sort of stuff is this?" she asked. "It's definitely not plastic."

"It looks a bit like a waxed jacket," Nuala replied, carefully unwrapping what seemed like yards of stuff.

The dormitory door opened and Josie called, "Come out the pair of you and admit defeat. We were right and you were wrong! Ha ha."

Nuala looked in amazement at Aileen and then at the pile of material on the bed. She put a finger to her lips at the same time pulling her quilt over all the mess. "Not a word about our find yet," she hissed in Aileen's ear.

"We're coming, Josie!" she called cheerfully. They hastily left the cubicle and joined Josie at the dormitory door.

"So you've found the famous Newgrange treasure, have you?" said Nuala smoothly. "Are we allowed to see it by any chance . . . "

"Yes," chimed in Aileen defiantly. "Produce the goods."

Josie looked at them. "Why all the hassle?" she asked. "That's why I'm here. We have it in the common room and I want to show it to you."

Exchanging puzzled glances, Nuala and Aileen followed Josie downstairs. Judith met them at the common room door and triumphantly handed a piece of paper to Nuala.

A bemused Nuala unrolled it and read out to Aileen:

"Ye treasure seekers of ye St Brigid's
Humble apologies and congratulations to ye
Third year maidens of ye college
Herein is your reward
Ye book of ye Boyne."

"Here's the book," said Judith smugly.

Nuala opened the book. It was made of stiff thick paper and entitled *Ye book of ye Boyne*.

"Look Aileen" she said, "each page has a cartoon drawing of someone. This one is called 'Ye gentle warriors of St Brigid's'."

Aileen peered over her arm and saw a drawing of six monsters wearing tennis whites and carrying racquets.

"It's the school tennis team," she giggled. "Turn over the page."

Nuala turned over and pointed out, 'Ye salmon of weirde knowledge.' "It's a salmon with the face of Mr Greene standing by a pile of *Jungle* cans," she laughed.

"Did you see one called 'Ye Bosse of ye Boyne'?" asked Judith.

Nuala flicked over the pages. "Ha ha, that's good, they're simply wicked, aren't they?" she grinned, showing Aileen a drawing of Sr Gobnait complete with veil and olive crown, sitting like a Roman emperor on a throne.

"What about our find?" whispered Aileen to Nuala. "Let's get to the dorm and find out."

Nuala nodded but the bell for tea rang just then. The common room cleared rapidly sweeping Nuala and Aileen along with them. Treasure-hunting was hungry work.

Never had tea seemed so long to the two friends. Eventually it was over and Nuala and Aileen were free to rush up to the dorm. As they raced up the stairs they could hear Gwendoline telling somebody in an excited voice that Natalie's mother was expected in St Brigid's on the following day.

Reaching the cubicle Nuala ripped off her quilt and pulled at the wax-like covering. Something wrapped in a sheet-like material fell on the bed. When Nuala peeled back this cover they saw revealed a hinged wooden box about twenty centimetres square.

"I feel nervous, very nervous," Nuala whispered to Aileen, who nodded.

"I know, just open it," she breathed tersely back.

Nuala undid the two tarnished clips and threw the lid back. They both gasped as they saw a fine wrought cover in front of them. Nuala picked it up gently.

"It's a book, Aileen," she said. "It seems to be made of some soft material and is simply beautifully illustrated. Just look . . . "

Aileen looked at the soft buff-coloured pages, covered in pointed script. "What sort of language is that? Look at those colours, it's simply fabulous!"

Nuala read out with difficulty, "'Prime,' that's Latin. It must be a prayer book."

Aileen looked at the book again. "It reminds me of that reproduction of the *Book of Kells* in the library, do you remember Sr Alice showing it to us last year?"

Nuala looked keenly at her. "If you're right, then it's priceless," she said as she carefully wrapped it up again.

Aileen nodded, "We've found a real treasure then. I can't believe it."

"Come on," Nuala spoke urgently. "We must show this to Sr Gobnait at once."

They found the tall nun in her office. As soon as she saw the book she sent for the librarian.

"Glory be to God," cried Sr Alice when Nuala opened the box, revealing their find. "You've found the stolen treasure of the Calfe's. Abbot Lynagh's *Book of Hours*."

20

The Lost Book of the Calfe's

"What a pain Sr Gobnait is not letting us tell anyone about you-know-what," complained Aileen bitterly to Nuala as they were walking back from the science lab, a few days later. "It's killing me keeping my mouth shut, especially as the others keep crowing over us about their cleverness in finding *Ye booke of ye Boyne* in Calfe's Pool."

"I know, it's driving me mad too," sympathised Nuala. "The hordes of reporters asking us questions that Sr Gobnait was worried about if the story leaked out couldn't be half as bad. On the other hand, think how silly they'll look when they hear about the real treasure we found in Carraigphooca, that'll shut them up fast."

"When is the expert coming from Dublin?" asked Aileen cheered up at the thought of Josie, Eithne and Gwendoline being shut up fast as they were the worst gloaters of the lot.

"I don't know, but it must be soon. Hush though, here's Judith," warned Nuala.

"Hi!" called Judith rather breathlessly as she caught up with them. "Did you hear the news?

Natalie and her mother are expected back today and Mrs Frossart wants to meet the whole year and thank us for our part in saving Natalie. Gwendoline has just told me."

"Brilliant. I'm just dying to hear the whole story and what they did with her wicked cousin and his friend," replied Nuala. "Not to mention the woman in pink and the mysterious Professor Jenkins."

"It sounds just like a thriller on TV," said Aileen, "especially as our own Steve was involved in the rescue too."

"Miss Crilly looked none the worse for her unexpected dip in the Boyne," commented Judith. "In fact she looked just the same as usual."

"All brisk and 'keep your mind on your work, girls'," agreed Aileen. "No wonder no one had the guts to ask her if she and Mr Greene were now an item."

"Wouldn't you too if you were her! All the same, wasn't it hilarious the way she got mad with him and then stepped back into the river. Then he, like a knight in armour or should I say a salmon, came galloping up and dived in to rescue her." Judith and Aileen started to giggle as the funny side hit them too.

"Salmon don't gallop," protested Judith. "They swim."

"Ye weirde salmon of ye Boyne," chuckled Aileen. "No wonder he dived, what else could a fish do!"

"Some people thought it was so romantic too,"

gasped Judith, almost overcome by the humour of it all. "You should have heard Monica gushing on about Kevin Costner and *The Bodyguard*."

"He'd better not see the *Ye booke of ye Boyne*," grinned Nuala, "not to mention 'Ye Bosse of ye Boyne.' She probably would start behaving like a Roman emperor then."

"That'd make some people feel a bit different about finding it then," sniggered Aileen, pleased at the thought of Sr Gobnait reacting to the clever ones.

They had reached the locker room by now, arriving in time to hear Gwendoline ask Monica if she had put her name down for the tour to Rome.

Monica nodded happily. "Mum is keen for me to see Rome," she explained, "and I've never been on a tour before."

"Brilliant. What about you, Judith?" asked Gwendoline. "I hear your cousins have their names on the list already."

"I don't know yet," Judith replied, looking enquiringly at Nuala and Aileen as she spoke.

"I don't think so," said Nuala. "The Rome tour is very expensive."

Josie who was standing in front of the mirror messing with her hair as usual murmured, "Should I cut it or not, that's the question . . . " Then she raised her voice, "Haven't we a weekend break coming soon?"

"We have," replied Monica who knew all the gossip as usual. "Sharon Kennedy is throwing a shorts and shades party on Friday night. She's invited the whole of fifth year to it."

"I wish I was in fifth year," said Deirdre enviously. "I'd just love to go to a shorts and shades party."

Nuala, Judith and Aileen left the locker room shortly followed by Josie. "One of the reasons I'm not fussed about going on the tour is that Sharon and her friend Lisa will be there. I can't abide either of them. Monica says that Sharon is determined to be head girl next year. I shudder at the thought," explained Nuala dramatically, suiting action to words.

"She couldn't be head girl," protested Josie. "They have to be serious and hard-working, keen on school spirit types. All Sharon lives for is a good social life."

"She's very matey with Sr Imelda," Judith pointed out as they walked up the stairs.

"You're right," agreed Aileen. "When the major was away, Sharon was always hanging around the office and doing jobs for Sr Imelda."

Gráinne was standing at the open door of the classroom when they arrived there. "Is it true or is it only a rumour," she asked, "about Natalie's mother wanting to speak to the whole class this evening?"

"Gwendoline says so anyway," replied Josie cheerfully. "It will be a nice break in our dull routine."

"I hope it won't be at *Together and Apart* time. I've missed at least three episodes already with all the fuss of Miss Crilly falling in the river and that stupid treasure hunt," complained Gráinne fretfully.

"Who needs *Together and Apart*," replied Nuala in a large-minded way, "when you're in the greatest soap on earth, *St Brigid's on the Boyne.*"

Even Gráinne had to join in the merry laughter which greeted this remark.

As it happened it wasn't Natalie or her mother who disturbed their viewing that evening but the expert from Dublin. Bronzed pony-tailed Todd, complete with surfboard, had barely started to plod across the sunny beach in their favourite epic when Nuala and Aileen were called away to the library. Everyone was so engrossed in watching the programme that not even Judith or Josie paid any attention to their departure from the room.

When they reached the library they found Sr Gobnait talking to an elegantly-dressed attractive looking woman.

"Come and meet Dr Madeline Brouder," said the nun. "I know you'll be pleased to hear that she confirms that you have indeed found the stolen treasure of the Calfe's."

"Yes indeed, and it has been a privilege to examine it," agreed the expert who had a very decisive way of speaking. Sr Alice, who was also present, led them over to a table on which had been laid in careful order the wrappings, the wooden box and the book itself.

"The wrappings are linen impregnated with oil which makes them waterproof, commonly known as oilskin. The inner wrapping is oiled silk, protecting the book from moisture and/or dust, which explains why it is in such good condition after nearly two hundred years in the hole in the rock."

"Whoever hid them obviously knew what they were doing," observed Sr Gobnait grimly.

The expert smiled and remarked, "It certainly looks like it."

She picked up the book and showed it to Nuala and Aileen, turning the pages lovingly as she did so. "It's so beautiful," she said. "Just look at that wonderful script and the soft calfskin pages, not to mention the intricately pierced cover of gold. It must have been a very special present to Abbot Lynagh."

"Why is it called a Book of Hours?" asked Aileen, after both of them marvelled at it too.

"You know that at certain hours of the day nuns and monks sing or say the Divine Praises? In the Middle Ages pious lay people recited prayers at certain hours in the day also. Until the printing press was invented all these books had to be written by hand, of course. They were in Latin until late in this century and, in the past, were commonly called *The Book of Hours*."

"I see," said Aileen. "I suppose it was stolen because it was so valuable."

"I don't know its history at that stage," said Dr Brouder, "but Sister Alice has promised to tell us what she knows."

"We don't know when or why the Calfes

acquired their treasure," started Sr Alice who had always been interested in the history of the castle. "It was around the end of the eighteenth century when Reginald Calfe decided to catalogue his library, the very room we are in. During the course of this process, which took ten years, they found the precious volume hidden somewhere among the books. There was great publicity and excitement about the find, and the Calfes discovered that anyone they had ever met wished to visit the castle to admire the book.

"Amongst them was a certain judge whom Reginald disliked. Somehow or other this man wrangled an invitation to visit the castle. He spent a week there and they say he spent his time either in the library or wandering around the grounds of the castle.

"Eventually he left for Dublin but he never reached it alive. His shocked family were told that he was shot dead by a highwayman who held up his coach, not an uncommon experience in those days.

"However, the legend quietly spread among the ordinary people that the fair young man on the white horse who held up the judge's coach was no robber, but a victim of the judge's prejudice in favour of false witnesses. In consequence the young man's family had suffered great losses over the subsequent unfair verdict. He challenged the judge to a duel, whereupon the unjust judge whipped out a pistol and fired at the young man, who had no option but to defend himself and retaliate in kind."

"How exciting!" cheered Nuala. "I hope he got away."

Sr Alice looked shocked but all she said was, "The following day the Calfes discovered their great loss and the book was never seen again until Nuala and Aileen found it."

"Are there any of the Calfe family left?" Sr Gobnait asked keenly.

The librarian shook her head.

"I must get some legal advice on our position then," was Sr Gobnait's immediate reaction. She got up from her chair. "It's time for study, Nuala and Aileen. Sr Alice, look after Dr Brouder please, I have to ring Mr Greene about a Boynepeace meeting. I won't be long."

Nuala and Aileen said goodbye, thanked the expert and hurried out of the library after Sr Gobnait.

"Excuse me please, Sister" Nuala said as they all walked along the corridor together. "I couldn't help overhearing what you were saying about Mr Greene. I really think that I should tell you that David, Aileen's cousin and his friend Paul were instrumental in helping us find the lost treasure of the Calfes."

As Sr Gobnait looked at her Nuala sought for a suitable way to tell her. "You could really call it a successful result of the Boynepeace venture and I think they should be allowed to see the book."

"That's simply splendid. I will tell Mr Greene to bring them over tonight. I have a feeling we'll have to give it to a museum in the end, unfortunately."

Aileen grinned at Nuala. "Sister Gobnait," she asked. "Don't say what it is, just tell them that we found the treasure and that it's a book. It will be a lovely surprise for them."

Sr Gobnait looked thoughtfully at Aileen. "I have a horrible feeling that I am being manipulated Aileen, but I'll do it – just this once."

"Oh thank you, Sister," they both cried as they went off to the study.

"That will give them a bit of a fright," said Aileen in a satisfied voice.

"Yes, I thought it might be good for them to learn some respect for 'Ye Bosse of ye Boyne'," laughed Nuala. "I suppose we can tell the others tonight too."

"Good," replied Aileen. "I'm looking forward to that."

21

Countdown

"There I was about to board a plane for Paris," declared Natalie's mother dramatically, "when Professor Jenkins turned up with the news that my father-in-law was seriously ill and that he had sent him to warn me that Natalie was in danger of being kidnapped by her cousins Aly and Mahmoud. You can imagine how I felt."

A week had passed since that eventful day when the same Professor Jenkins, assisted by Steve the tennis coach, had prevented Natalie from actually being kidnapped by Mahmoud and Annaliese Phibbs.

Now Mrs Frossart was sitting in the school garden surrounded by the whole of the third year, who were listening avidly to her side of the story.

"I didn't know what to do," she confessed, continuing the saga. "Then I remembered Legs. She was always so competent and reliable, even when we were at school. So I contacted her. She suggested Natalie would be safe here, and so it was arranged."

None of her listeners quite liked to ask who the

mysterious 'Legs' was. Fortunately Natalie had no such reservation. "Who is this 'Legs'?" she asked impatiently. "I've never heard of her before."

Her mother, elegant in a beige linen suit, laughed ruefully. "Oh dear, whatever made me call Sr Gobnait that. I haven't done so for years. She was called 'Legs' at school because she was always competing in running and hurdling events, and winning them too."

A ripple of amusement passed through her listeners. Amongst the half-smothered giggles Monica could be heard whispering loudly to her neighbour, "Imagine Sr Gobnait was known as 'Legs', what a joke!"

"So we smuggled Natalie over here," continued Mrs Frossart smiling at the girls' reaction to Sr Gobnait's nickname, totally unconcerned about her friend's feelings in the matter. "And Professor Jenkins followed, pretending to be after fish in your river."

"If Natalie was smuggled over, how did they find out that she was here?" asked Gwendoline, who was sitting in the front row, next to Natalie.

"I don't know, but I have since discovered that Perdita Remor who had worked for Natalie's grandfather, was in league with Aly and Mahmoud. She must have ferreted out the information somehow," was Mrs Frossart's reply.

"How did Professor Jenkins get involved, is he a detective, a kind of PI?" asked Aileen.

Mrs Frossart laughed. "No, he really is a professor. I think he has been a friend of Natalie's grandfather for years. He asked Steve to help him after he came upon Perdita in the village. I don't think he took the kidnapping story seriously until then."

"She must have been the woman in pink!" cried Nuala. "Do you remember, Josie? I saw them talking together the day we went down the village for the ice creams."

"I remember that, you were afraid she was after you," confirmed Josie.

Nuala then told about her experience in the museum, explaining that she had thought at first that the woman in pink had indeed been after her, that day in the village.

"Poor Nuala, what a horrible experience," said Natalie's mother. "Maybe that's the reason she brought her sister Annaliese Phibbs in to take her place. She may have been afraid you'd recognised her."

Nuala shook her head. "She didn't see me then, but she might have thought I recognised her after they came to the school pretending to be parents, which I did."

"What happened to Mahmoud and Annaliese after Professor Jenkins hooked them that day?" asked Josie.

"Well, the professor and Steve took them to Dublin and handed them over to the police there. However, Natalie's grandfather and I didn't want any fuss or publicity over the whole incident, so the charges were dropped. Both of them went back to England. Grandfather, who is now fully recovered, met them there. He assures me that he has dealt with them and we will have nothing further to worry about in future," replied Natalie's mother in a very grim voice which made them wonder what Natalie's grandfather had done to the would-be kidnappers. Nobody liked to ask.

Mrs Frossart rose from her chair. "Girls, I want to thank you from the bottom of my heart," she said in a voice of such sincerity that nobody was in any doubt that she really meant it. "Only for you, my dearest Natalie would have been kidnapped by a pair of rogues, and probably made marry another one. I think Natalie's hair is a very small sacrifice to pay for this. Anyway it will grow again."

"We all think she looks great with her hair cut short," chimed in Gwendoline loyally.

Mrs Frossart laughed and replied "I do too, but it's up to her whatever way she wants to wear it. I would like to show my gratitude in a more concrete way. When Natalie comes back from seeing her grandfather I intend giving you a really big party and presents, of course. I have already given Sr Gobnait a cheque towards the swimming pool. Natalie has told me of your difficulty there."

"Three cheers for Natalie and her mother!" called Gráinne.

"Hip hip hurrah!" The response was deafening.

Just as the cheering came to an end Sr Gobnait appeared on the scene, all smiles. It appeared that Professor Jenkins had arrived to accompany the two Frossarts on their way to Dublin Airport.

When they were gone Nuala, sinking

comfortably into the chair which Natalie's mother had just vacated, voiced her feelings. "That's what I call a good term. Plenty of excitement, followed by a big party and presents."

"True," agreed Judith. "What a term we've had, what with kidnapping, treasure hunts and even a teacher falling into the Boyne in front of us."

"Don't forget my brilliant birthday party on the castle roof, not to mention the awful storm that night," interrupted Nuala.

Aileen, sitting on the grass and leaning against Nuala's chair, lazily watched the rest of their class drift back to the castle chatting animatedly. "I think the best part was finding the lost Book of the Calfes," she said reminding Judith and Josie of that great feat. "I laugh whenever I think of David and Paul all polite and nervous meeting Ye Bosse of ye Boyne and trying to think of some way of explaining away *Ye Booke of Ye Boyne*."

"If only they had known that she was also Ye Legges of ye Boyne," laughed Josie.

"It was a bit cruel of you, Aileen," reproved Judith, "giving your cousin a fright like that."

"Cruel my foot. David and Paul enjoyed the joke as much as we did – afterwards of course," replied Aileen energetically. "Think of the good that came out of the treasure hunt – not only did we find the *Book of Hours*, but David says that Mr Greene has given away his fishing rods and goes whistling happily around Newgrange College all the time."

"You're not serious!" chuckled Josie. "What does Paul think of that?"

"He is only disgusted," grinned Aileen. "Look, here's Gwendoline back. Natalie and her ma must be gone."

"Nuala," called Gwendoline hurrying across the grass towards the four girls who were the only ones left now. "Sr Gobnait wants you in her office at once."

"Whatever does she want me for?" asked Nuala, startled into jumping up from her chair. Gwendoline shook her head.

"She didn't say, but she looked in great humour."

"We'll all go with you," suggested Judith. "And she won't have the nerve to give you any trouble."

Nuala laughed. "You'll only have to utter the magic word 'Legs' and she'll crumple up at your feet," she said as she started walking across the grass, closely followed by the others.

They had almost reached the door of the castle, when Aileen gave a shout and grabbed at her throat.

"My chain!" she cried. "My good silver chain, it's gone. I know I had it when we were all sitting around Mrs Frossart."

"Don't worry, Aileen, it's bound to be on the grass there," said Josie soothingly. "Come on, I'll go back with you and help in the search."

Judith and Gwendoline wanted to help too, but in the end they went ahead with Nuala while Aileen and Josie hurried back to look for the chain.

They hadn't been searching long when Josie gave a triumphant shout.

"There it is, Aileen," she cried. "Just behind the leg of that chair Nuala was sitting on," and she pointed to where Aileen herself had been sitting earlier that afternoon.

Aileen bent down and peered at the grass. The chain lay in a tiny heap. Thankfully she picked it up. "You're brilliant, Josie," she said gratefully. "I don't know how you spotted it. Thanks a million."

"Don't mention it," smiled Josie. "It was a pleasure."

Then they hurried back to join the others. When they reached the office corridor they could see a crowd of girls talking and laughing at the notice-board.

Aileen was so curious to know what all the excitement was about that she hailed the first person they met, who happened to be Sharon Kennedy.

"What's all the fuss about up there?" she asked eagerly.

Sharon stopped and looked at them unpleasantly. "If Nuala didn't bother telling her friends," she sneered at them, "why should I?" Then she walked right past them without another word.

"What's biting her?" asked Aileen in amazement.

"I don't know," replied Josie making an expressive face back at her.

Judith broke away from the crowd around the notice-board. Waving excitedly she ran to meet Aileen and Josie. "Isn't it fabulous news about Nuala?" she called as she came up to them.

"What news?" asked Aileen impatiently.

"Didn't Sharon tell you? The mean pig. It's just that Nuala's won first prize in the Heritage competition with her *Canticle of a Chalice*."

"Hooray, hooray," cried Aileen. "Now she'll probably come on the tour to Rome."

"Brilliant!" echoed Josie as they ran up to the board to see the good news for themselves.

Also by Poolbeg

Bad Habits at St Brigid's

By

Geri Valentine

It's the new term at St Brigid's. The pleasure of meeting old and new friends is spoiled by the news that the popular Sister Clare is away on sick leave for at least a year and that the school will be run by the cold and remote Mother Borgia and the nasty snooping Sister Mercy. Nuala and Judith, the new girl from London, combine with Aileen, Josie and the twins Fidelma and Eithne, to form a secret society called Crime Busters to investigate mysterious happenings about the school. It is Judith who first suspects that the spate of robberies in the area is somehow connected with the noises and strange lights that have made St Brigid's a very spooky place after dark. It seems hardly likely, but could someone living in the school be involved?

Bad Habits at St Brigid's is a great book – full of suspense, excitement and larks!

Also by Poolbeg

New Broom at St Brigid's

By

Geri Valentine

St Brigid's, that unusual girls' school situated in a castle by the Boyne, is again the scene of mystery, excitement and fun.

There's the new head, Sr Gobnait, younger and tougher than the mysterious Mother Borgia. However, the old gang of Nuala, Ju, the twins and the rest have other things to interest them. There's a prehistoric ice-house, a ghost and secret passages, and a very sinister clinic.

The fun and thrills never slacken: *New Broom at St Brigid's* is a super sequel to *Bad Habits at St Brigid's*!